DANGEROUS ODYSSEY

Jane Edwards

Chivers Press • G.K. Hall & Co.
Bath, Avon, England Thorndike, Maine USA

This Large Print edition is published by Chivers Press, England, and by G.K. Hall & Co., USA.

Published in 1996 in the U.K. by arrangement with the author.

Published in 1996 in the U.S. by arrangement with Jane Edwards.

U.K. Hardcover ISBN 0–7451–3989–2 (Chivers Large Print)
U.K. Softcover   ISBN 0–7451–3999–X (Camden Large Print)
U.S. Softcover   ISBN 0–7838–1620–0 (Nightingale Collection Edition)

The text of this Large Print edition is unabridged.
Other aspects of the book may vary from the original edition.

All the characters in this book are fictitious, and any resemblance to actual persons, living or dead, is purely coincidental.

Set in 16 pt. New Times Roman.

Printed in Great Britain on acid-free paper.

British Library Cataloguing in Publication Data available

Library of Congress Cataloging-in-Publication Data

Edwards, Jane (Jane Campbell), 1932–
    Dangerous odyssey / Jane Edwards.
    p.   cm.
    ISBN 0–7838–1620–0 (lg. print : lsc)
    1. Large type books.   I. Title.
[PS3555.D933D36   1996]
813′.54—dc20
                                                                95–48829

DANGEROUS ODYSSEY

This book is for one peach of an editor,
Barbara J. Brett

DANGEROUS ODYSSEY

FOREWORD

Except for such historical personages as Lord Elgin and Süleyman the Magnificent, all the characters in this book are imaginary. The background, on the other hand, is factual, and the story of Priam's treasure absolutely true.

It would be unjust not to acknowledge a debt of gratitude to art historian Alexander Eliot for his fine article, 'The Greek Island That Blew Apart ' (*Travel & Leisure*: July, 1974). There, Eliot gives a vivid description of Santorini, past and present.

I am even more indebted to Irving Stone's biographical novel, *The Greek Treasure* (Doubleday, 1975), which tells of the spectacular discoveries made by Heinrich (whom Stone calls Henry) Schliemann, with the help of his wife, Sophia. In the 1870s, during an era when archaeology was largely a science of untested theory, this couple used the descriptions in Homer's *Iliad* to locate the site of historical Troy.

Excavations revealed that nine different cities, each bearing that name, were built in the same place over the centuries. The priceless artifacts unearthed by the Schliemanns are attributed to Troy VII, which, according to the *Iliad* and to Virgil's *Aeneid*, fell about the year 1184 B.C. They were brought to Berlin, and for

1

several decades afterward they were exhibited there in the Museum for Early History.

In his Author's Note at the end of *The Greek Treasure*, Mr Stone warns that anyone hoping to have a look at these antiquities is doomed to disappointment. During the closing days of World War II, with the Russian army thundering toward the gates of Berlin, the museum's curators bundled up the gold and either hid or buried it in an effort to keep it safe. To this very day, not a single item from that exciting trove has ever reappeared.

It is fascinating to speculate about what might have happened to the treasure. What follows is my version of one possibility.

—*Jane Edwards*

CHAPTER ONE

Whenever Kelsey was upset, she baked. From scratch. Norwegian style, if it was a case of serious anger—that mad-as-a-wet-hen kind of rage—and too bad about calories or cholesterol. The process involved real creamery butter, fresh eggs, triple-sifted confectioners' sugar, exotic spices. The rich resulting batter was molded into the old-fashioned cookie presses her great-grandmother had brought all the way from Oslo early in the century, when emigrating to the Pacific Northwest as a bride.

Given Tucker's scathing tirade, this old-fashioned, hands-on activity seemed particularly fitting today. 'Victorian,' he had termed her rejection. 'Obsolete.' 'Paleozoic.' And finally, flaunting seven years of higher education, 'Antediluvian.'

Still smoldering, Kelsey squeezed out *spritz* pinwheels in a satisfactory pattern across the Teflon baking sheet. She made a grimace of annoyance when the phone started to ring, but in her present frame of mind the racket could be endured just so long. On the third strident peal she reached out with a flour-dusted hand and grabbed the receiver.

'No!' she snapped. 'Absolutely not!'

A moment's stunned silence met this

3

negative decree. Then her cousin Joanna's voice began making soothing noises. 'It's only me, Kelse. Are you out in the kitchen, baking Grandma Helga's cookies?'

'How did you guess?' Kelsey gave an embarrassed half laugh. She stretched the cord of the wall phone to its elastic limits while crossing the room to set the oven to preheat. 'I'm sorry for shouting in your ear. Foolishly I jumped to the conclusion that you were Tucker, calling to apologize. But even groveling wouldn't have done him any good. We're through. Finished. Kaput!'

'Hold the thought,' Joanna pleaded fervently. 'What massive favor did he want this time—for you to actually sit down and write his doctoral dissertation for him, after already having done most of the research?'

'No,' Kelsey said, although in truth hints had more than once been cast in this direction. 'He wanted to move in.'

'Why does that surprise me? Probably because he waited so long. After all, it's a full ten days since your roommate got married and went off to live in Connecticut. Did he also offer to shoulder Doreen's half of the rent? '

'He didn't have the chance. Once I said no, he was too busy pointing out that my attitude belonged back in the Dark Ages.'

'Ha! He's the one who's behind the times. This is the nineties, not the seventies. Commitment is back in style in a big way.'

4

Before Kelsey could reply that commitment was one word Tucker Grant seemed never to have heard of, she caught the rumble of an insistent male voice in the background. At once Joanna's tone changed from matey to businesslike.

'It's interesting that you should mention that spare room in your apartment, Kelse, because that's part of what I wanted to talk to you about. I have a client in my office, a man, and—'

'Are you out of your mind?'

'—and his seven-year-old niece,' her cousin continued imperturbably. 'We're hoping you may be able to help us solve a problem.'

Kelsey eyed the litter of mixing bowls and utensils strewn across her counter. 'I'm sorry, Jo, but I already have my hands full. By the time I got this mess cleaned up and jumped on the Metro, your office would be closed.'

'We'll come to you. Twenty minutes. Put on the coffeepot.'

With the dial tone buzzing in her ear, Kelsey was given no opportunity for argument. She shoved the pan of cookies into the oven, then filled the ten-cup coffee machine and set the switch to 'brew.' If Joanna's client was one of those wimpy types who insisted on decaf, he was out of luck, she thought crossly.

Then she stopped to laugh at herself. That hadn't sounded like a wimpy rumble in the background. Far from it!

As she washed her hands and tidied up the kitchen, it occurred to Kelsey to wonder what they wanted with her. Jo had referred to the man in her office as a 'client,' making the mention of a seven-year-old niece follow quite logically. Her business was highly specialized, furnishing capable nanny/escorts for children who had considerable distances to travel—and whose parents or guardians were able to pay some hefty fees to ensure they didn't have to do so alone.

Once or twice in the past Joanna had tried to urge Kelsey to accept an assignment herself. 'You have the ideal qualifications for the job,' she'd pointed out. 'As a teacher of gifted children, you're used to dealing with precocious youngsters from September through May. Why not make the most of your long summer vacation? Treat yourself to a fully, paid trip and earn some extra money besides.'

'Because when I finally do have a chance to see more of this wide, wonderful world, I want to do it in depth,' Kelsey had replied. 'Not holding a sticky little hand and reading *The Little Engine That Could* all the way across the Atlantic before turning around and coming straight home again.'

The under-ten group she worked with at one of Seattle's most prestigious private schools were brilliant students. They had been enrolled to have their horizons enhanced and their thirst for learning and creativity stimulated.

There was no doubt in Kelsey's mind that rewarding travel experiences of her own would turn into marvelous teaching material to share with her class.

Early this year, with her master's degree earned and enough saved to finance two glorious if budget-priced months in Europe absorbing Old World culture, magnificent art, and inspiring architecture, she had applied for her passport and started making plans. Then just last month her roommate had met the man of her dreams, a magazine photographer visiting the West Coast on business. Their wedding had followed a whirlwind courtship. Now, instead of a close friend to share travel as well as living expenses, Kelsey was faced with financing the rent on the Queen Anne Hill apartment all by herself. She hoped that by September she could find another congenial female to take Doreen's place. But reservations for that long-awaited trip had had to be canceled. Without someone with whom to split the costs—

Kelsey frowned as she untied her apron. Why had Joanna mentioned her spare room in the same breath with the client's young niece? Her business was to provide nannies to escort children on trips, not to find them lodgings here at home.

She wasn't given long to ponder the question. Minutes later she was opening the door to her cousin, a tall, attractive young

7

woman whose Viking genes, like Kelsey's own, showed in her coloring and bone structure. Joanna was trailed inside by a dark, broad-shouldered man. He clung reassuringly to the hand of a dainty little girl.

'Hello.' Kelsey stooped down, placing herself on the child's level. One glimpse of that small, stiff face and her heart immediately went out to the girl. Before either of them could say another word, a buzzing noise from the kitchen interrupted.

'Time to take the second batch of cookies out of the oven.' Straightening up, Kelsey included the two adults in her explanation, but reserved her smile and an invitation for the youngster. 'Want to come and help me?'

Shy brown eyes sought those of the man. He nodded permission. 'Go ahead, Zoe. They smell terrific.'

His voice was deep. Interesting. Kelsey glanced his way for a split second before turning and heading for the kitchen with Zoe at her heels. Children's names tended to go in cycles. At the moment her students included a lopsided number of Jennifers and Tiffanys. Zoe, she decided, was refreshingly different. Greek, wasn't it? With her honey-colored ponytail and fair skin, the child didn't look Greek. Her uncle certainly did, though. A Mediterranean ancestry was clearly evident in the glossy black hair curling thickly across his well-shaped head, in the smooth olive skin and huge, long-lashed dark-brown eyes.

For one quick look, that was a lot of noticing, Kelsey thought wryly. She pulled her mind away from Joanna's client to reach for a pair of padded oven mitts. Knowing that children liked nothing better than to take an important part in whatever was going on, she pointed to a metal rack on the counter. Would Zoe please bring it over to the table, while she herself removed the baking sheet from the oven?

'Okay now, hold it steady. I'll use the spatula to scoop these off so they can cool.'

'They're awfully yellow,' Zoe observed critically. 'Are you sure they baked all the way through?'

Kelsey laughed and complimented Zoe on her perceptiveness. 'Norwegian cookies are supposed to look pale and lemon colored. They'll be fine once they've had a chance to set. Now let's brush the tops with a drop of beaten egg white and decorate some with cinnamon candies and the rest with almonds. While we're doing that, maybe your uncle and my cousin would like to come sit down and have a cup of coffee.'

'I thought you'd never ask.' The two adults had been hovering in the doorway. Joanna stepped into the cozy kitchen and performed introductions. 'Kelsey Anderson, meet Michael Devos.'

He took a deep, appreciative breath of the tantalizing aromas mingling in the air. 'I can't decide which smells better, the coffee or the cookies.'

Hadn't she assured herself that he wouldn't be the kind who drank decaf? Kelsey unhooked four blue mugs decorated with geese from the little wooden stand on the counter. She filled the first one with milk, then poured hot black coffee into the others.

Michael Devos didn't miss Zoe's pleasure at being handed a mug of her own rather than a babyish glass. He watched her finish pressing almonds in a decorative pattern, then gravely accepted the slightly mashed cookie she handed to him.

'Wow!' he said, savoring the taste, making a big deal out of it for her sake. 'Oh, wow! You two can bake for me any day.'

For the time being, at least, the tense, troubled look had vanished from the little girl's face. Delighted to be acting as cohostess, she passed the cookies to Joanna while Kelsey brought over paper napkins, then slid into the fourth chair, next to Zoe's uncle.

The man was almost sinfully good-looking. Usually gorgeous hunks with lots of muscles were so conceited they didn't appeal to Kelsey. With Michael Devos, however, not a single word or gesture gave any indication of his being a male impressed with his own attributes. He was comfortable with himself, that was all. So self-confident, in fact, that it hadn't seemed to bother him in the least that at five-foot-ten she was exactly the same height as he. Instead, those expressive brown eyes had stared straight across into her blue ones, as if attempting to assess her character rather than worry about what she thought of him.

He wasn't much older than she was, either. Twenty-seven or eight, maybe, to her twenty-six. Even so, he looked like a man with a lot on his mind. Serious stuff.

Kelsey had no more than formed the thought when she saw him glance with loving protectiveness toward his small niece, then shift his gaze to Joanna. Deliberately, as though they had a prearranged set of signals all worked out, he nodded.

Without a moment's hesitation Joanna looked up and said, 'Kelse, Michael has an important matter he'd like to discuss with you. It's, uh, sort of complicated. If the two of you went out and had something to eat, it would give you a chance to get acquainted. Zoe and I can stay here and order in a pizza.'

Kelsey had the oddest feeling that she'd stumbled into the middle of a conspiracy. Somehow she was involved—or would be, if these two had their way. She looked narrowly from one to the other, all set to declare that she had no desire to play their little game, whatever it might be. Still, she and Joanna had been inseparable friends since childhood. Her cousin would never pull a dirty trick on her. And while the man practically radiated tension, his concern was fully focused on his niece. It was as though he were afraid of something, for Zoe's sake—trying to shelter her while keeping the precautions low-key so she wouldn't catch on.

Dark eyes lingered on Kelsey's wary face. 'Please,' he said. 'I'll explain as we go, but there isn't much time. I'm due to be on a plane to Rome in four hours.'

Rome! The very name conjured up a bouquet of visions in Kelsey's head. The Colosseum. The Trevi Fountain. St Peter's, the Via Veneto, the Spanish Steps. All those fabulous places she'd read about in a dozen guidebooks. And she'd be willing to bet he didn't mean to visit even one of them.

She opened her mouth, then closed it again. Instead, she nodded. It couldn't hurt to find out what this was all about. Outside, it had started to drizzle. Suitably murky weather, she decided, to go along with a highly murky situation.

'I'll get my coat.'

Neither of them said another word until after they had emerged from her apartment building and turned south, heading toward the site of a long-ago World's Fair and which had since become an impressive center for arts and sciences. Neither of them paid the slightest heed to the lacy white arches visible from ten blocks over, or to the Space Needle hovering above that part of town like a tall, knock-

12

kneed UFO.

'You were wonderful with my niece back there,' Michael said. 'Your cousin tells me you teach. Exceptional children, is that right?'

'My students tend to be particularly bright, yes.' Kelsey raised a blond eyebrow, determined to garner a few facts for herself before answering any more questions. 'What do you do, Michael?'

He jammed his hands into his pockets and increased his pace along the glistening sidewalk. 'My two partners and I run an international air-taxi service. Our seaplanes fly on a regular schedule from Elliott Bay here in Seattle, north to a half dozen port cities in Canada.' He added that the three of them were all former jet jockeys, Navy pilots who had flown F-14 Tomcats and A-6 Intruders off the carrier *Nimitz*.

His sideways glance caught the surprise in Kelsey's expression. 'What's the matter? I don't look like a pilot?'

Involuntarily her gaze dropped to the wide shoulders beneath his lightweight jacket. 'I think I would have pegged you as a boat person myself.'

'Not a bad guess. That's how I was brought up, diving from a boat off the Gulf Coast of Florida. My father is a sponge fisherman down in Tarpon Springs. He still can't figure out why I prefer the air to the sea.'

Michael forged across the intersection just

13

as the light was changing. In the next block the neighborhood changed from residential to commercial. From the corner on down, shops alternated with restaurants and other small businesses.

He looked over their choices, then left the decision up to Kelsey. 'What'll it be? Seafood? Chinese? Or a burger and fries?'

'In the fish place they hover, and the noise level is so high in the hamburger joint, it's necessary to use sign language to carry on a conversation. Better make it Chinese,' she concluded. 'That *is* what you wanted, right? A spot to talk?'

In response he opened a door decorated with a jade dragon and stood back to let her enter.

Ten minutes later the waitress had taken their order and vanished, leaving them to face each other over small porcelain cups of pale-green tea.

'All right,' Kelsey demanded. 'What's going on?'

Michael's reply was equally direct. 'My sister and her husband have disappeared.'

'Zoe's parents?' Kelsey warmed her hands with the cup. Serious stuff, indeed. No wonder he hadn't once cracked a smile. 'Where was she when they dropped out of sight?'

'En route to Florida. Out of the blue ten days ago my folks received a cablegram from Ione, asking them to meet Zoe at Miami International. She said her daughter would be

14

carrying a letter that explained everything.'

'Did it?'

'Up to a point.' Michael shot a glance at his watch. 'Maybe I'd better sketch in the background.'

Ione, his sister, was six years older than he, Michael said. She held the position of professor of classical studies at a small college in Jacksonville. Her husband, Rupert Strasse, was a writer who studied ancient civilizations. 'In his books he attempts to connect the mythology surrounding a specific region to the actual lifestyles of the people who inhabited the area.'

'That must be fascinating, trying to separate truth from legend, then show how one affected the other. It sounds as if your sister and her husband have a lot in common, professionally.'

'In every way. They're the most compatible couple I've ever known. I hope someday to have a marriage as solid as theirs,' Michael said. 'My parents are fond of Rupert too, though it took them a while to accept Ione's choice of a husband. Greece was their beloved homeland. That country suffered greatly at the hands of the Germans during World War II.'

With a name like Rupert Strasse, Kelsey figured there wasn't much doubt about the ancestry of Zoe's father. 'Was he born in Germany?'

Michael nodded. 'Yes, though he's been an

American citizen since he was a kid. His mother and father died in a train wreck when he was quite small. A childless American major and his wife who were stationed in Frankfurt adopted Rupert, brought him to the States, and gave him a good education.'

The waitress arrived with the spicy Szechuan food they had ordered. Michael waited until she was out of earshot before continuing.

'It wasn't until about two years ago that Rupert met up with distant relatives, quite by chance, and developed an interest in learning more about his birth family. One of the facts he stumbled on intrigued him more than all the rest. Most of his mother's family had been killed in the bombing, but her grandfather was employed as an assistant curator at the Berlin Museum for Early History toward the end of World War II.'

Back in a far corner of Kelsey's mind the name of the museum rang a bell. She couldn't immediately put her finger on where or how she might have come across information about such a place. More than likely through a stray fact footnoted in some college textbook. Unlike Zoe's parents, she was a specialist in very young children, not in very old history. Nevertheless, there was *something* ...

'That must have been a desperate time, with Berlin bombed into rubble and conquering armies flooding into the city from all directions,' Kelsey remarked.

16

She took a forkful of Mongolian beef and swallowed, not really tasting the food. Trying to remember what there was of special importance about that museum made her feel as if she were groping her way down a long, dark tunnel. Any minute now a glimmer of light was bound to come to her. If she followed it to its source, she'd understand what Michael was talking about.

But she wasn't really sure she wanted to know any more. Whatever this was all about had put a troubled look on a little girl's face. It had the man across the table from her worried sick. She glanced up. He was watching her trying to puzzle it out. Almost against her will, she said, 'The people responsible for keeping those ancient artifacts safe must have been concerned that they might be destroyed.'

'Or stolen,' Michael agreed. 'The advancing Russian soldiers wouldn't have cared how many thousands of years old those plates and buttons and death masks might be, but they'd certainly know gold when they saw it.'

'Who wouldn't! Michael, are we talking about the treasure that German archaeologist what's-his-name—'

'Heinrich Schliemann.'

'Yes, that's right; the fabulous trove Heinrich Schliemann and his Greek wife Sophia dug up when they discovered the site of Troy back in the 1870s? *Priam's* treasure?'

A conspiratorial glint sparkled in Michael

17

Devos's dark eyes. Clearly he was delighted that there was no need to explain the unique significance of the objects that had once been on display there in East Berlin.

'The very same. Unfortunately nobody has seen the stuff since the spring of 1945. The people in charge of that museum bundled up the treasure into a number of packages mere hours before the Red Army troops entered the city.'

A lump the size of a baseball seemed to be blocking Kelsey's throat. 'Nobody knows what happened to all those priceless things?'

Michael shook his head. 'The treasure was carted away for safekeeping in the dead of night. Maybe it was hidden. Buried. Who knows? But in all these years not a single gold bead has ever surfaced.'

'Then why,' she asked wonderingly, 'was Rupert Strasse so intrigued by the fact that one of his relatives had been associated with the museum?'

'Because he managed to trace the old man's later movements. Survivors scattered. Many more lost their lives in that panic-stricken rush to leave the ruined city. But Rupert is a skilled, persistent researcher. Also, through his adoptive father he had access to all sorts of generally unavailable documents that had long since been filed away in military archives. He discovered proof that his great-grandfather had made it safely into the American sector.

Then, toward the end of the Occupation period, he left Germany and never returned.'

Kelsey thought about the stories she had read. 'Where did he go? To South America?'

'No,' Michael said. 'He headed for Greece.'

CHAPTER TWO

For a moment Kelsey was speechless. Then she exclaimed, 'For Greece!'

'Surprised?' Michael's handsome mouth curved in brief amusement. Then his expression quickly grew serious again. 'It was the Nazis who fled to South America, hoping to escape retribution at the end of the war. Paul Dürer was just an ordinary little man who worked in a museum. He seems to have been something of a classical scholar. Checking back through his university records, Rupert came across a mention of Herr Dürer's ability to read the works of Homer in the original Greek. But he had less success in earning a living. By all accounts, he was more of a dreamer than a doer.'

'Then it's all the more astonishing that he should have set off on such a long trek. Germany and Greece are a tremendous distance apart.'

Over the past few months Kelsey had studied numerous maps of Europe. While

19

planning an itinerary, she had run her fingers across the globe so often there were worn spots on its rounded surface. Even though her long-awaited trip had been shelved, all that familiarization with geography now let her speak with assurance.

'Those first few years after the war must have really been chaotic,' she went on in a pensive tone. 'The Russians were playing grab-a-country, and millions of people were searching for what was left of their families. Especially in Germany, the cities had been bombed into rubble. People had a hard time finding a place to live or enough to eat. It wouldn't have been possible to just—just go on vacation, would it?'

'Not for an elderly man with barely ten marks to his name,' Michael assured her. 'Paul Dürer was past seventy and in frail health when he received permission to travel from the Allied Zone of Germany into France. The doctors had given him only about a year to live. They hoped he might do better in a milder climate.'

'So he started out ... how?'

'By train.' Michael grimaced, thinking of the hardships that must have been involved in that journey. 'He hadn't any money for the fare. But in a letter he wrote back to his former landlady after arriving in Marseilles, he said he'd been allowed to ride for nothing in the baggage compartment.'

'Marseilles,' Kelsey breathed. 'A seaport right on the Mediterranean.'

20

'One of the busiest. Israel had become a nation just a couple of years earlier. Can you imagine the vast numbers of survivors from all over Europe who must have gathered there, clamoring for passage to the Promised Land?'

She could almost picture the turmoil ... the desperation.

'With all that going on, Paul Dürer not only managed to stay alive but to wangle a berth on a rusted old scow bound for Italy and beyond. The wait, combined with the voyage itself, took months.'

'How did he live in the meantime? Then, too, the fare can't have been cheap. You said he didn't even have money enough for a train ticket, and yet...'

Michael displayed great interest in his prawns, mixing sesame seed with the hot Chinese mustard and dipping a large shrimp into the spice before taking a bite. 'He didn't. But in Marseilles he arranged for the sale of two or three objects of value.'

There were several possibilities as to how he could have come by those things, Kelsey told herself. For example, someone could have died and left him their furniture. That sounded like a pretty farfetched explanation, though.

'Rupert didn't find out about that until later,' Michael said, evading a direct question for the moment. 'He had trouble securing proof that it was really his ancestor who booked passage aboard that tramp steamer.

21

The ship's manifest listed nobody named Paul Dürer among the passengers. A Paul Duval was aboard, however. According to the log, the crew's doctor treated this man Duval for the same type of heart ailment that Paul Dürer had been diagnosed as having.'

By now Kelsey had given up all pretense of trying to eat. 'He changed his *name?* Why on earth would he have done that? Oh! Because a German wouldn't have been welcome in Greece so soon after the war?'

'That's certain to have been at least one of the reasons. Dürer spoke excellent French,' Michael went on. 'Once he was in that country, it shouldn't have been too difficult for him to pass himself off as a citizen of France who had lost his identification papers and needed to have his travel documents reissued.'

Millions of people who'd never had passports before would have been applying for them at about that time, Kelsey thought, remembering what Michael had said about refugees jamming the seaports. 'That sounds logical,' she admitted. 'So let's take it for granted that Rupert's great-grandfather did leave Marseilles on that steamer, only now he was posing as a Frenchman named Duval. The end of the line was—where?'

'The ship's single port of call in Greece was a small town on the mainland across the strait from the island of Corfu. Paul Duval went ashore at Igoumenitsa. A large steamer trunk

22

debarked with him.'

A sharp, swift glance showed Zoe's uncle sitting there looking as innocent as a first-grader. Watching him polish off another prawn, Kelsey had an idea of how a donkey must have felt, plodding patiently along after a dangling carrot. Michael was throwing out one intriguing hint at a time, with a view to getting her more and more engrossed in the fascinating tale he was spinning. She already knew that he wanted something from her. Right now he was using up precious minutes in an effort to pique her interest so fully that she'd be unable to refuse whatever he asked.

Kelsey resented being manipulated. On the verge of jumping up and stalking out of the restaurant, she darted another look at her companion's face. The anxious expression lurking in the depths of his dark eyes stopped her. Michael wasn't leading her on for fun. He seemed convinced that her help was desperately needed.

She settled back down in the chair. 'All right, Michael. I'll bite. What was in the steamer trunk?'

'I don't know.'

'I'll bet you could make a pretty accurate guess, though. Wouldn't the baggage of people entering Greece be inspected?'

'Not necessarily. For one thing, drug smuggling wasn't the atrocious problem then that it is nowadays. The trunk was heavy, but if an elderly scholar wanted to bring in a few well-thumbed reference books to study as he traveled from one classical site to another, why should anyone care?'

Customs officials would have cast a far more careful eye on anything being taken out of the country, Michael added. During the five long centuries when Greece was under Turkish rule, many priceless works of art had been removed from the ancient ruins and taken away to other parts of the world. Now stiff penalties were assessed on anyone attempting to remove even an icon, let alone larger works of art.

'But who would suspect anyone of trying to bring treasures back *in* to their country of origin?'

'You believe that's what Paul Dürer set out to do?' Kelsey asked in an awed tone. 'That this long, hard trip was a—a—'

'Pilgrimage?' Michael gave a sober nod. 'That was Rupert's conclusion. He became so involved in the whole idea that he suggested Ione apply for a sabbatical so she and their daughter could accompany him to Greece. Professors are sometimes allowed to do that, you know—take a year off for study and travel. The idea is that they'll be better teachers when they return to the classroom.'

'Yes, I'm familiar with the practice.' Kelsey tried not to sigh. She'd had a small-scale version of the same idea in mind for herself this summer, but unfortunately it hadn't panned out. 'What did your sister think about the suggestion?'

'Ione was excited about the possibilities, even though she realized they'd be following a forty-year-old trail. Neither she nor Rupert believed it would be easy to find out what the old man did or where he went after arriving in Greece.'

But if necessary they were willing to take a year out of their lives to try and find out, Kelsey reflected. They wouldn't have done that unless they were convinced the answers might prove to be of vital importance.

A sudden thought crossed her mind. 'Michael, you mentioned that while he was in Marseilles, Paul Dürer sold some things. Were they—'

A couple walked past, following the hostess toward a vacant table down the aisle. 'No, they weren't.' Michael's hasty interruption warned her to watch what she said. 'That transaction did involve items that had come from the same place, though.'

'The museum?'

Her question was the merest whisper. Relieved by her discretion, Michael nodded. 'Uh—huh. Small things. Easy to carry. The fact that he waited years to dispose of them, even though he might often have gone hungry in the meantime, reinforced Rupert's belief that the old man had a definite goal he was determined to pursue. He felt his great-grandfather considered himself to have been charged with a sacred trust. Not only did he need needed to make sure no harm came to the artifacts he'd been given to guard, but that he set out to return objects to Greece that never should have been taken away in the first place.'

'But Troy is in Turkey, isn't it?'

'It is now. In ancient times, however, the Aegean coast of Asia Minor was closely related to the Greek civilization,' Michael pointed out. 'Dürer was a classical scholar. He'd have known that, even though he never had the opportunity to travel in his younger days and see the remains of the Golden Age for himself. He also knew he hadn't long to live. I imagine he'd have been very reluctant to let someone else have the satisfaction of fulfilling his goal.'

'Even if he could have found a person who was absolutely trustworthy.' Kelsey tried not to think of the mind-boggling value of the treasure that had been whisked away from Berlin's Museum for Early History barely in the nick of time. Just the current value of the gold alone would have been immense.

But if Paul Dürer really had been safeguarding the objects Rupert believed he'd had in his possession, the items in that steamer trunk would have been molded of precious metal more than three thousand years in the past. They'd be part of a deathless legend. A treasure beyond price.

No wonder the old man had attempted to

maintain such a low profile, Kelsey told herself. He would have had more than one reason for changing his name. Paul Duval was quite literally a nobody—he had never really existed. Paul Dürer, on the other hand, could have been traced back to that museum. If the right person's suspicions were aroused—

She swallowed hard. 'Before their disappearance were your sister and brother-in-law able to find out anything?'

'Enough to intrigue them. By then, of course, the trail was stone cold. Another difficulty was that in Germany and France, Rupert had traced old written records, using them as a helpful resource. No such help existed in Greece. Also, he had trouble with the language at first, though naturally Ione and Zoe spoke it well. But in the course of asking hundreds of questions—'

'Naturally?'

'Oh, yes.' Michael looked up and gave an emphatic nod. 'The national feeling is extremely strong. It's a poor land, and ancestors sometimes had no choice but to emigrate. No matter where they live, though, every child of Greek descent learns the native tongue and the traditional songs and dances. The heritage is never allowed to die out. So yes, naturally, Ione would have taught Zoe at home, just as our parents instructed us when we were children growing up in Florida.' He grinned. 'You haven't lived until you've heard

27

Greek spoken in a Southern drawl.'

'I'll bet.' The radiance of that sudden smile warmed Kelsey; it was like having the sun come out and touch her with its rays. She watched with reluctance while it faded. 'Go on, Michael. I realize you're pressed for time, but you've gone too far now not to tell me the rest of it. What did they discover?'

Faint pointers had indicated that an elderly man who spoke with the dignity of Plato and Aristotle had traveled across the rocky, mountainous land in a peasant cart pulled by a mule. Whenever possible he stayed a night or two at a remote monastery while zigzagging up one side of Greece and down the other.

'So Rupert and Ione visited the monasteries too, as well as every place else they could think of. It was a frustrating process, trying to trace his ramblings forty years later, but they kept plugging away at it,' Michael said. 'Every evening the three of them would talk over what they'd learned since morning. They'd pore over the maps, planning the next day's route. And Ione drew maps herself. Late last month the trail led them to Athens.'

Kelsey didn't miss the sudden tightening of his lips. 'What happened there?'

'My brother-in-law checked the family into a hotel, then went to collect some mail that was being held for him at a branch of his publisher, just off Omonia Square. There he ran into an old colleague who suggested they go have a drink together at a sidewalk café.'

Alec Westerlin, the man Rupert had encountered, was considered quite an expert on Etruscan jewelry and art and had written several books on the subject. 'He told Rupert that he'd been hired to authenticate a couple of rings that a wealthy man was interested in acquiring for his private collection. Westerlin was offered a bonus if he could dig up a provenance on them. And guess what?'

Rings, Kelsey thought. Small items. Easily transported. 'I'll bet he learned that they were once exhibited in a Berlin museum that was overrun by the Russians in 1945.'

'Right the first time. It wasn't a Russian who sold them, though. Westerlin resurrected an old museum catalog. It had group pictures of the staff in the back. An antique dealer in Marseilles picked Paul Dürer's photo out from all the rest.'

'If I were a wealthy collector who was interested in choice antiquities, I think I might have started wondering what else that former museum employee might have smuggled out of Germany with him.'

'I'm glad you aren't working for the other side,' Michael complimented her. 'Westerlin told Rupert that his client insisted on having him continue the investigation after he'd learned where the rings came from. He was rewarded with another bonus when he reported back that he'd traced Dürer as far as

Athens.'

'Did he say who'd paid him?'

'I think he might have, but my brother-in-law didn't pass any names on to me. Rupert did say that Westerlin had been sloshing down the *ouzo* pretty steadily. He'd had enough of the job, he insisted. What he really wanted to do was head back to Italy so he could get started on the research for a new book. That morning after collecting his money, he'd told his employer he was through. That someone else would have to pick up the trail if he wanted to learn any more details.'

The expression on Michael's face half prepared Kelsey for what was coming next.

'Suddenly Westerlin seemed to realize that he'd said too much. He drained the glass of *ouzo* and said he had to run, that a travel agent across the square was holding an air ticket for him. Rupert was fishing drachmas out of his pocket to pay the waiter when he heard a shout from the people at the next table. Just as Westerlin was preparing to step off the curb, a speeding car roared forward. Two of its wheels swerved right up on the sidewalk. It plowed into Westerlin, then kept right on going. So did Rupert, as soon as he realized the man he'd spoken with only thirty seconds earlier was dead.'

'I'd have been terrified!'

'He was. It seemed all too clear that Westerlin had been cold-bloodedly eliminated

30

to prevent him from passing on whatever he'd learned to anyone else. And here was Rupert, along with the wife and child he adored, involved in the same quest that had suddenly turned so dangerous.'

'No wonder he and Ione decided to send their daughter back to America in a hurry!'

Michael nodded. 'Within hours Zoe was aboard a Pan Am flight bound for Miami. The letter in her pocket had been written in a hurry, but it contained all the details I've just passed on to you. Rupert and Ione walked out of the Athens airport as soon as Zoe's plane was off the ground. They haven't been seen since.'

'Do you think—'

'I don't know. But I'm going to find out.'

The implacable resolve in his voice gave Kelsey goose bumps. She didn't like to think of him getting mixed up in a high-stakes treasure hunt that had already cost the life of one man. And maybe, by now, of Zoe's mother and father too. She hadn't forgotten the tight, scared look on the little girl's face.

'Why is Zoe here in Seattle with you now, instead of back East with her grandparents?'

'Because she wasn't safe there,' Michael answered grimly. 'Four days after she arrived in Florida, a van pulled up in front of my parents' home. The man behind the wheel kept the motor running while his cohort jumped out and ran up to the porch where Zoe was playing. He clamped an arm around her and started hauling her toward the street. Thank God there was an alert teenager out watering the lawn next door. He heard her scream and turned the hose full-force on the kidnapper. The guy was so stunned he just dropped her and ran.'

But that had been only the opening incident. 'Two nights later the dogs set up a howl. Someone was trying to jimmy the back door. That was enough for Papa. He put in a call to me while Mama got Zoe up and dressed and packed her clothes. Then the three of them drove to the marina, cast off, and headed out to the Gulf.'

The following afternoon Michael landed a pontoon plane alongside his father's sponge-fishing boat. After a quick conference he took off again, with Zoe aboard.

'Before leaving the West Coast, I gave our reserve pilot a call and arranged for him to fly my air-taxi schedule until further notice. Then I told my partners that an important family matter had come up and that I wouldn't be back until everything was taken care of.'

From the sound of it, that was likely to be a while. Kelsey felt a surge of admiration for the man seated across the table. When his parents and niece had needed him, he had simply dropped everything and come to their assistance. She tried to picture Tucker Grant reacting in such a way, and failed miserably. The one big interest in his life was Tucker

32

Grant. But for Michael Devos, family loyalty headed his list of priorities.

'Weren't you worried that whoever had traced Zoe to Florida might learn that she also had an uncle here in Washington?' she asked.

'Darned right. That's why I haven't been near either my apartment or the office since I made that cross-country trip. A couple I know lent me their cabin over on Bainbridge Island. We've been staying there the last couple of days while I've been trying to find out what happened to my sister and brother-in-law. They're the same people who recommended your cousin's nanny service to me.'

Michael directed his steady gaze toward Kelsey. 'When I realized there was no chance of tracing Ione and Rupert from halfway 'round the world, I went to see Joanna and gave her a sketchy rundown of the situation. I told her I needed someone absolutely trustworthy to look after Zoe here in town for a week or so. Then—possibly—bring her to me in Greece. She said there was only one person she knew dependable enough for a job as sensitive as this one. You.'

So now it was all out in the open. Kelsey knew that Michael had risked a great deal by laying his cards on the table as he'd done.

'I'm flattered. Truly, I ... How good of you both to put your faith in me like this.' She hoped she wasn't going to spoil her reliable image by bursting into tears. 'Michael, I'll be glad to keep Zoe here with me for as long as she needs to stay. That's no problem. But to suggest bringing her back to Greece and putting her within reach of whoever ordered that hit-and-run driver to wipe out Alec Westerlin—How can you even consider exposing her to that sort of danger again?'

'Because she isn't going to be safe anywhere until this business is resolved.' Some of the tension had eased out of Michael's broad shoulders as soon as Kelsey had offered her help. Now he leaned forward, wrapping her hands in his large, capable grip and speaking so intently that she knew he must have been mulling over these convictions for days.

'Whoever wanted Zoe kidnapped has the wealth and power—and the lack of scruples—to conduct a worldwide search for her. He obviously believes she knows where her parents have gone. To tell the truth, so do I.'

The warmth flowing from his fingers to hers made Kelsey all too aware of his male vitality. Had the subject they were discussing not been so urgent, she would have had trouble making her own pulse behave.

'Because they always discussed the search with her?' she asked. 'Spread out the maps and talked things over as a family?'

'Exactly. With our clan it's a case of "all for one, and one for all." I have a hunch that by the time they reached Athens, Ione and Rupert had a pretty shrewd idea of where the quest was headed. It would have been openly debated among the three of them. Then, when they sent Zoe away, they must have told her it would be safest if she forgot everything they'd talked about. Zoe's done her best to block it all out. So far she hasn't even opened up to me. But that's one smart little girl back there in your apartment. And if I'm not successful in picking up her parents' trail by myself, I'll need her to give me a hand in finding them.'

Michael added that by hitchhiking to Europe on a military transport plane, he was hoping to keep his departure from the USA under wraps.

'From Rome I'll hop a bus over to Brindisi, then take a ferryboat across to Corfu. This time of year at least a million tourists from Northern Europe are heading down to the shores of the Mediterranean for their summer vacations. If I'm lucky, I can get lost in their midst, slip into Greece through the back door, without anyone being the wiser.'

His voice was intent, dead serious. 'If I find I can't do the job alone, will you bring Zoe to me, Kelsey? Don't worry about money. I'll leave plenty with Joanna to cover all her expenses and yours too.'

'I have a little saved,' she was astonished to hear herself volunteering. What had happened to her qualms, her determination not to become involved? In just an hour her reservations had done a complete about-face.

35

'If you run short—'

'Thanks, Kelsey. It shouldn't come to that, but it's impossible to predict in advance what sort of resources will be necessary. If I need you to toss a few drachmas into the kitty, I'll ask, okay? Meanwhile I'm enormously relieved to know we'll be working toward the same goal.'

He laid some money on the waitress's tray to cover the cost of their meal. Then he took Kelsey's hand again, leading the way out of the restaurant. 'The rain's almost stopped. Come on. On the way back to your place we'll work out a way to keep in touch without placing Zoe—or you—in jeopardy.'

CHAPTER THREE

Any transatlantic phone calls, they decided, should be made to Joanna's home number. In that way, no one could trace a link between Michael and Kelsey. This simple precaution would also keep her cousin's business from being openly connected with a man who might have reason to seek an escort for a small child.

Michael worried most about how contact was to be established within Greece, in the event things went that far. 'The time may come when I'll need to send you a message by way of somebody else. You must have solid assurance that the communication is actually from me before following through on whatever instructions it contains.'

The dampness had turned his hair into a tousled thatch of glossy black curls. He could have posed for a classical statue, Kelsey thought. Theseus, perhaps, who'd vanquished the Minotaur. Or maybe Paris, who had stolen Helen and spirited her off to Troy.

She gave a sudden shiver, jerked back to reality by the recollection of the treasures found on that site and the memory of how they had disappeared. An awareness of her companion's extraordinary good looks was thrust aside, along with any inclination to view this latest possibility—that she might be lured into a trap—as part of a thickening plot from an old Hitchcock movie. Unfortunately, nothing about this situation involved make-believe.

'It sounds melodramatic, but maybe we'd better agree on a password,' she suggested. 'Something easy to remember.'

'Good idea. It also has to be devious enough to keep an adversary from using it to his own advantage,' Michael added to her suggestion.

Out in Puget Sound a ship's foghorn reverberated, warning another vessel out of its path. The Navy was an important presence in western Washington. Like most local civilians, Kelsey was fairly knowledgeable about the fleet. She was used to watching the huge gray ships steaming in and out and to seeing the contrails of military planes overhead.

Hearing the deep blare gave her an idea. 'Didn't you tell me you used to fly jets off an aircraft carrier? The A-6 Intruder and the F-14 Tomcat, right?' She turned her head, liking the fact that his steady gaze was on an exact level with hers. 'How about starting off any message you send by saying, "The Intruder is on the flight deck"?'

'Perfect,' Michael agreed. 'For safety's sake, let's carry it one step further. If anyone should contact you verbally with that statement, challenge it by asking what sort of Intruder. Unless they reply that it's the F-14, that message did not come from me. Okay?'

'Agreed.' Reversing the designations of the two types of planes was a simple precaution, but a good one, Kelsey thought. She brought up another point that had occurred to her. 'If Zoe and I do wind up in Greece, should we pretend to be ordinary tourists?'

'I can't think of a better cover, can you? Especially since it's not just Americans who head for Greece in droves every summer. The islands are a popular vacation spot for people from all over Northern Europe.' Michael's lips curved in reluctant amusement. 'Scandinavian women, in particular. There'll be thousands of girls around with long blond hair and wide blue eyes, just like yours. Except that most of them won't be anywhere near as pretty.'

They had arrived at Kelsey's apartment

house. Michael held the door, then followed her inside. In the foyer he paused instead of moving at once to the stairway.

'You're taking a lot on faith, Kelsey, and I'm grateful. Helping out like this is—well, above and beyond what anyone ought to be asked to do for strangers. I've been wondering ... Is there ... anyone who's likely to resent—'

'Being left high and dry if I should decide to fly off to Europe at a moment's notice?'

Under other circumstances Kelsey might have giggled. Sailors had quite a reputation for glib tongues and full-steam-ahead tactics. Not many former Navy flyers would have been so hesitant about asking if she were involved with another man. Quickly she reminded herself that in spite of his flattering compliment moments earlier, Michael Devos wasn't personally interested in her. He just needed to make sure no stumbling blocks were likely to interfere with the safeguarding of his niece.

She shook her head. 'No. That is, I *have* been dating someone fairly regularly for almost a year now, but—'

There seemed to be no tactful way of admitting that her former beau was a charming, lazy freeloader, the sort of opportunist who'd pace off seven leagues if anyone offered him an inch. Tucker had taken it for granted that she would be willing to drift along indefinitely, smoothing out life's little wrinkles for him, while never expecting more than a casual 'Thanks, babe' in return. But the worm had finally turned. This morning—good heavens, was it only this morning?—she had run out of patience with his 'me first' attitude.

Michael didn't have time to listen to the details of their huffy spat, however. All he wanted from her was the assurance that she would take good care of Zoe.

'But we've recently decided to call it quits,' she concluded mildly. 'As for my helping out, why don't we just consider it a mutual favor? My original vacation plans fell through, and I'm not due back in the classroom until September. Zoe's a sweetheart. She'll be good company. Taking care of her is bound to be more fun than teaching summer school.'

Michael regarded her thoughtfully for a moment longer. Then he extended his hand and proceeded to seal their bargain with a shake. 'Sounds like a good deal to me, Kelsey Anderson. I'll try to make sure you never regret becoming involved with the Devos family.'

*   *   *

Fully experienced in dealing with gifted children, Kelsey soon realized that her young charge was exceptionally bright. Zoe could read and write in two languages—and they involved different alphabets! She spoke with confidence about becoming an archaeologist when she grew up. But a more immediate dilemma was definitely on her mind. It finally came to the surface after they'd been together for a week.

'Uncle Michael said he was going away to look for my mommy and daddy,' the little girl proclaimed unexpectedly.

The two of them had made avocado sandwiches, pressing the wheat bread into interesting shapes with an assortment of cookie cutters. Though Zoe usually had a good appetite, she sat at the table now, swinging her feet and barely nibbling at her lunch. Her small face looked doleful, even more troubled than it had on the first day they'd met.

'He told me that he might need my help,' she went on. 'Those special maps my mom drew—he says it's important for me to remember everything about them I can. But, Kelsey, Daddy didn't *want* anybody to know where they were going. He said they 'spected to be gone for a little while and that I was s'posed to keep real quiet about all the things we'd talked about together.' Big brown eyes regarded Kelsey pleadingly. 'What do you think I ought to do?'

Kelsey hid her shock by turning to put the milk carton back into the refrigerator. So Zoe *did* know more than she'd been letting on! And now her seven-year-old conscience was tearing her apart. She loved and trusted both her father and her uncle, yet to her they seemed to be working at cross purposes. She didn't know how to handle the apparent contradiction.

'That's a hard, grown-up decision you're trying to make.' Kelsey slid into her own chair, letting Zoe know by her tone and expression that she was taking the problem seriously. 'One of the things that has your Uncle Michael so concerned is that your dad and mom planned on being gone for only a little while, as you said. But they still haven't shown up. Nobody's heard from them since they put you on that airplane.'

Zoe shook her head morosely, her ponytail bobbing up and down. 'He's afraid of some bad man tracking them down. The same one who tried to find out where Great-great-grandpapa Paul took the steamer trunk.'

The words were scarcely out before the little girl clapped a hand over her mouth, aghast at having let this bit of information slip. Hastily Kelsey reassured her that she already knew most of the story.

'It's all right, sweetheart. I'm on your side. And yes, I think you're right. That *is* what's worrying your uncle.' *Among other things*, she added to herself. 'He told me that you and your parents used to talk things over every night while you were in Greece. He thinks those maps you saw held a clue as to where they planned to go after leaving Athens.' She reached across the table, taking the small hand in hers. 'Things don't always work out the way we hope, honeybunch. By now your dad and mom are likely to really need your uncle's help. Michael was going to try to find them by himself, but if he can't, he wants us to come give him a hand. Would you be willing to do that?'

Zoe thought it over for a minute or so. Then she gave a decisive nod. 'Yes. I think we'd better.' She looked soberly up at Kelsey. 'Did you know that somebody tried to kidnap me? What if it happens again?'

This child was a realist, Kelsey thought in admiration. In fact, she was a lot more willing to face facts than many adults would have been. 'I've been thinking about that myself, Zoe,' she admitted. 'That's the main reason we've been sticking so close to home all week. But if we *do* have to do some traveling, we had better find you a disguise.' She picked up a sandwich, encouraging Zoe to do the same. 'After lunch let's get out the hairbrush and comb. We can try braiding your hair and pinning it on top of your head.'

Half an hour later she was forced to concede that the new hairstyle didn't do much to change Zoe's appearance.

'I don't think that does much good, either.' Critically the little girl peered into the mirror after they'd unplaited the braids and arranged her hair to lie loosely over her shoulders. 'Maybe we should just cut it all off and pretend I'm a boy.'

Kelsey caught her breath. Out of the mouths of babes!

'That's a fantastic idea. But you have such pretty hair. Wouldn't your mother have a fit?'

'Not if it kept me from getting kidnapped,' Zoe pointed out with practical good sense.

'Well, I certainly approve of keeping one's priorities straight.' Thoughtfully, Kelsey eyed her pint-sized houseguest. Zoe was so petite that she appeared younger than her true age. Dressed as a boy, she'd probably look no more than five. 'We'd need to think of something to call you,' she said. 'Hold on a sec'. I'll be right back.'

Soon afterward Kelsey slipped back into her apartment and replaced the chain lock. 'My friend Catherine next door is expecting a baby,' she explained, dropping down on the couch next to Zoe. 'She and her husband have been hunting through this book of names to decide on the ones they like best. Let's look at the choices. Try to pick out something you wouldn't mind answering to, just in case it becomes necessary.'

The project kept the little girl busy the rest of the afternoon. Kelsey was setting the table for supper when she heard the book slam shut. A moment later Zoe marched into the kitchen with a resolute look on her face.

'I'll be Jason,' she announced.

'That's a nice name. Very popular too. How come you picked it instead of something fancy,

44

like Bartholomew or Sebastian?'

Zoe giggled. 'Oh, Kelsey, you're just teasing me! You remember who Jason was, don't you? He's the hero of one of my favorite stories.' Her voice dropped to a conspiratorial whisper. 'Jason went off to find the Golden Fleece!'

*   *   *

Joanna was in the habit of calling up several times each day to make sure they were all right and that there was nothing they needed from the store. It came as no surprise, therefore, when the phone rang an hour after they'd finished the dishes. But as soon as Kelsey heard her cousin's guarded tone of voice, she knew this wasn't just another casual contact to see how everything was going.

'What's up, Jo? Has something happened?'

'Yes, I just finished a *very* long-distance conversation. Michael Devos says he needs Zoe there, Kelse. He's been working with several trusted friends, but they've run out of leads. How soon can the two of you be ready to leave for Athens?'

Kelsey thought fast. If they headed for the barber shop first thing in the morning, then continued on from there to the boys' department of the nearest department store, they should be set to go by noon. 'Tomorrow afternoon soon enough? I can get most of the packing done this evening. But listen, Jo, when

45

you call Michael back, better warn him that he's in for a surprise.'

'You'll have to spring it on him yourself, I'm afraid. He didn't leave a number where I could get hold of him.'

Joanna said that before his departure Michael and she had agreed on a schedule and route for the travelers, to eliminate the need for discussing details over the phone. 'He's planning to meet you himself at Hellikon Airport in Athens, when your plane gets in from London. But if he can't follow through on this plan or even leave a message there, you're to go directly to the hotel and wait to be contacted. It's a place called the Acantha,' she added, somewhat dubiously. 'I've never heard of it, but he assured me it's very clean and respectable.'

Kelsey recalled her discussion with Michael about blending in with the Scandinavian tourists. 'I'm sure it will be, Jo. Chances are it caters to European vacationers rather than to Americans. That's likely to make it safer for us.'

'Listen, Kelse—you're not getting cold feet, are you?'

'You said yourself it's impossible to get hold of Michael. Would it do me any good if I were?'

*   *   *

'Have a look down there. This part of the

Alps is known as the Dolomites. Not my favorite view, by a long shot. I'm always happy to be safely past.'

Peering out at the forbidding gray-and-white landscape far below, Kelsey saw granite peaks, jagged and threatening, jutting up through glacial blankets of ice. Between them lurked deep, shadow-filled crevasses. If eidelweiss or other wildflowers grew down there, they weren't visible from this altitude. Nor was there any sign of an Alpine village like those charming clusters of chalets they had occasionally glimpsed while droning over Switzerland.

Clouds floated beneath the airliner's wing, curtaining off this harsh view of Italy's northernmost border. Drawing her gaze back inside, Kelsey reflected on how lucky they had been to draw such a congenial seatmate. Sarah Twelvetrees was a redheaded Englishwoman, tall and slender, and dressed in the last word of fashion. In her early thirties, she had a career that sounded fascinating—traveling around the world, acquiring art objects for a prestigious London gallery.

'I much prefer warm, sunny spots to mountains,' Sarah went on in that clear, pleasant accent that reminded Kelsey of Julie Andrews doing Mary Poppins. 'The gallery has a branch in Antigua, so much of my time is spent in the West Indies. Fortunately, since I'm seldom home to mingle with the neighbors, that infamous British reserve was omitted from my makeup at birth. Wherever I'm headed, I enjoy making friends with the people I meet en route.'

'What a lovely pastime!'

Much as she enjoyed the other woman's company, Kelsey kept her replies to Sarah's chatter brief. It seemed like weeks since they'd left home, instead of less than a day. The first half of the trip had involved a smooth polar flight from Seattle to London. At Heathrow Airport she and Zoe spent an hour stretching their legs while the destination tags tied to their luggage were changed from cards reading LHR to others marked HEH in large black letters. This accomplished, they transferred to one of the large modern jets belonging to Olympic, the national airline of Greece, for the second long hop of the journey.

Once aboard, Zoe had curled up and fallen asleep immediately. Kelsey yearned to do the same thing, but she was too keyed-up to relax. There was no telling what lay ahead, she warned herself. She'd have to be prepared for anything. Or, worse still, nothing. Michael might meet her on arrival and order her to turn around and go right back where she'd come from.

She rubbed her tired eyes. The drastic time change was beginning to take its toll. If she could have managed to rest, the jet lag would have been easier to keep at bay. But there didn't seem much chance of that with the Englishwoman in the aisle seat.

For the first hour of the flight Sarah had spent her time gazing around at their fellow passengers. The gallery's clientele was a large one, she explained; she hated to risk offending a well-to-do patron by failing to notice him or her. But after Kelsey asked whether people in that income bracket wouldn't be sitting up front in first class, Sarah agreed that she was probably wasting her time.

Upon learning that this was her seatmate's first trip to Europe, Sarah appointed herself unofficial tour guide. With a pang of regret Kelsey looked down at the elegant French châteaus passing under their wing and later got a bird's-eye view of Bavaria. How she had looked forward to seeing Heidelberg and the Black Forest! But from a somewhat closer perspective than thirty-five thousand feet in the air!

Eventually the sparkling blue Adriatic came into view, then the red rooftops of the old walled city of Dubrovnik. As she looked ahead to Greece, Sarah's prattle focused in on what was evidently her favorite subject.

'Shopping for practically everything is best in the modern sections of Athens,' she remarked, while conceding that the *Plaka*, or old city, was the place to browse for books. 'For myself, I never can resist gold trinkets handcrafted in the ancient Greek style. Even nowadays they're a real bargain. The two best jewelry shops are both on Panepistimiou Street.' She glanced across at the snoozing child occupying the window seat. 'Your boy wouldn't be interested, of course, but if you're bringing gifts home for little girls, try Hellas Dolls. Each of their creations is costumed in authentic native dress.'

'It all sounds marvelous,' Kelsey murmured after listening to Sarah enthusiastically recommend Sistovaris Frères for furs and rave about the smart fashion accessories to be found at the boutique of Ioannis Tseklenis. 'I'm afraid simply learning to pronounce those long Greek names will be an achievement in itself. Besides, sight-seeing will take up most of our time. We'll have to wait and see how far the travelers' checks stretch before going overboard on souvenirs.'

When the Englishwoman got up to visit the lavatory—the 'loo,' she called it—Kelsey checked Zoe's seat belt, making sure it was still loosely fastened. Then she slanted her own chair back to a more restful position. How wonderful it would be, she thought, if shopping and sight-seeing among the ancient ruins were really to be her only concerns in the coming days.

Closing her eyes, she clung to the belief that everything was going to work out all right. Encouragingly enough, one major hurdle already seemed to have been overcome. After one casual look at Zoe's cropped hair and sturdy denim clothing, Sarah had jumped to the conclusion that 'he' and Kelsey were mother and son.

The disguise was good, though hardly foolproof. Still, unless one of them got careless, there was no reason why the masquerade shouldn't work perfectly.

Kelsey felt a twinge of fear at the possibility of their simple little smoke screen being penetrated. The stakes were much too high to risk any slipups. Their unknown nemesis had taken swift, ruthless steps to eliminate Alec Westerlin before he could broadcast what he'd learned. Clearly, the person behind the brutal hit-and-run believed that Paul Dürer had smuggled a collection of priceless antiquities into Greece many years earlier. He was prepared to go to extreme measures to secure those objects before anyone else could announce their discovery.

During the past ten days concern for Zoe's safety had seldom been out of Kelsey's mind. The child's security as well as that of her parents was on the line. Michael's too. Her own skin as well, more than likely, she reminded herself now. She was in it with them, right up to her neck. A great deal was riding on a simple deception contrived to keep a little girl's identity secret.

An hour later Sarah slid her elegant Gucci bag out from the seat ahead and grumbled at the prospect of a long wait at the baggage carousel to collect the rest of her luggage. Hearing these remarks from an experienced traveler made Kelsey all the more pleased that she'd packed so lightly. Everything they'd brought along had been stowed into the soft-sided case and canvas knapsack that had fit neatly into the compartment above their seats—and that she could carry herself, in a pinch.

'Been nice meeting you,' Sarah said, stepping into the aisle before others from the rear could crowd ahead. 'I'd offer you a lift into town, but the man who's to meet me usually drives a two-seater.'

'No problem.' Kelsey was just as glad they were going their separate ways, now that the plane was on the ground. Sarah was nice, but it would be awkward greeting Michael with her along—especially when she tried to explain how the dainty little niece he'd been expecting to see had come to be transformed into a boy clad in Levi's, striped T-shirt, and high-top tennies. 'Maybe we'll bump into each other again at one of those boutiques you mentioned. Good-bye.'

At the end of a half hour in Hellikon Airport, Kelsey was forced to admit that at least one of her worries had been needless. There'd been no need to fret about witnesses to her meeting with Michael, because he hadn't shown up. After their passports had been stamped, their baggage checked and chalk-marked, she went in search of a message. There was none.

Nothing. Her heart sank as she turned away from the counter. No Michael, no word from him. What could have happened?

But for Zoe's sake she couldn't afford to let her apprehension show. There was no need to panic, anyway. She knew where to go. Fatigue curled through her body as Kelsey and her small companion trudged out of the busy terminal. A hot bath and a refreshing nap were neck-and-neck contenders for the top of her wish list. Much as she longed to head for the hotel without further delay, though, caution kept her from hailing a taxi. The driver might remember someone as tall as she. Someone whose coloring instantly marked her a foreigner. Someone with a child in tow.

The bus would be better. On it, they could slip into the city without being noticed.

One of the smelly diesel rigs bound for Constitution Square and other central destinations in the Greek capital was perched at the curb, starting to load. Kelsey added their luggage to the heap beginning to accumulate, paid for two places with a fistful of the drachmas she had purchased before leaving Seattle, and asked that they be dropped off in the *Plaka*. She climbed aboard, settled Zoe in the aisle seat, then sat down next to the window where she could keep a watchful eye on their baggage.

It was then that she noticed the short, swarthy man in the checkered shirt for the first time. There was little to distinguish him from the hundreds of other males who had crisscrossed her path since arrival. Still, the elaborately offhanded way he sidled up to the stack of luggage nudged her attention.

Cardboard tags scrawled with the letters HRH, the internationally designated symbol for Athens' Hellikon Airport, fluttered from every bag in the stack. Leather tags also dangled from the handle of her suitcase and from Zoe's knapsack, but Kelsey had prudently marked these only with her initials. Now, seeing the avid interest with which the man scanned each piece of luggage at the curb, she was suddenly very glad she had thought to take this small precaution.

The last suitcase thumped into the massive storage compartment. As the driver slammed down the hatch, the loiterer stepped back. Instead of ambling off, though, he squinted up at the large panoramic windows framing each seat. Before Kelsey could turn her head, the sharp gaze focused on her.

And stayed.

A frisson of apprehension trembled up her spine. She swung around, thankful that Zoe was tucked in the aisle seat where she couldn't be observed from outside. Moments later the rumbling engine signaled that the bus was ready to depart. As it started to move, Kelsey gathered her courage and glanced outside once again. The man who had stared at her so disconcertingly had vanished.

Relief broke out in a sigh. What a scaredy-cat she was getting to be! What had she expected—that he would swagger aboard and attempt to snatch away the child? Next she'd be suspecting wrongdoing from the pair of robed and bearded Orthodox priests seated catercorner across the aisle, or from the elderly woman back in the corner, swathed in a heavy black scarf despite the oppressive heat!

Fishing in her shoulder bag, Kelsey pulled out a pair of dark glasses. Anyone would squint on such a glary day as this. Here in Greece the light was intense, flooding mercilessly down from the hot blue sky.

Greece, she exulted to herself, where democracy had been born. Where Western civilization had begun. Where the first Olympic Games had been staged nearly eight centuries before the birth of Christ.

Greece. She was here!

'Here,' she had to admit as the bus rumbled onto the expressway, at the moment resembled one of the less attractive portions of southern California. The sere, treeless hills were dappled with sagebrush, and the passing traffic kicked up an appalling amount of dust. Obviously there had been no rain in months. Trying to accustom herself to such an uninspiring landscape was rather a shock to someone coming from lush, evergreen Washington.

But not nearly so rude a shock as encountering the swarthy man with the squint again. When the bus rumbled to a halt in a noisy, crowded section of the city where the streets were scarcely wider than alleyways, the driver beckoned to Kelsey. This, he indicated, was her stop. She and Zoe stepped off behind two other travelers and waited while their bags were unearthed. At once the driver hopped back aboard, the bus's horn blaring as he swung into traffic. The massive vehicle just missed piling into a string of cars headed in the opposite direction.

The spectacle of raised fists and shouted insults was considered entertaining by the other pedestrians. Kelsey paid no attention, however. She found herself staring almost in panic at the battered Renault that had dodged up to the curb not ten feet from where she stood. In the driver's seat a man's checkered shirt stood out in stark relief against the dazzling light of the street.

Her desperate glance darted first in one direction, then the other. As she swiveled, she caught a glimpse of a tall, vertical sign marking the three-story building across the street. Stylized letters spelled out the word *ACANTHA*.

The hotel! Could they reach it before he intercepted them?

Kelsey grabbed Zoe's arm, snatched up both knapsack and suitcase, and bolted.

CHAPTER FOUR

Once Kelsey and Zoe were through the hotel's solid double doors, street noises faded to a low hum. Shutters closed out the glare and pushed back at the formidable afternoon heat. Better yet, the slatted window coverings prevented prying eyes from peering inside.

Sanctuary! In early times fugitives at the end of their rope had fled to a church in a last-ditch attempt to gain freedom. Kelsey knew exactly how they must have felt when they stumbled over the threshold to safety.

'What's the matter? Why are we running away?'

Zoe had tugged her arm free and was staring up in bewilderment. Kelsey's conscience gave a twinge. People were depending on her to act like a calm, capable, professional adult—not like a rabbit who panicked at the sight of her own shadow!

Depositing the luggage on the patterned Persian carpet, she sank down into one of the lobby's capacious chairs and snuggled the child on her lap. 'I'm sorry if I frightened you,' she murmured, straining to get her quaking self under control. 'Guess I must be awfully tired, otherwise I'd be coping a lot more sensibly.'

She was all too well aware that for a moment out there in the street her poise and good judgment had both come perilously close to deserting her. Had she been alone, she might have behaved differently—stood her ground and challenged the man who had trailed the bus here to this unfashionable quarter of town. But Zoe's safety was her primary concern. She'd acted promptly on instinct to remove her from danger.

Though the little girl was still waiting patiently for an explanation, Kelsey hesitated, reluctant to give her the idea that there was anything to fear. Very seldom had a cloud shadowed her own carefree childhood. Times were different now, unfortunately. As a teacher she knew how essential it was to educate even tiny tots about the hazards of drugs, to warn them of the ease with which an abductor could whisk them away from home and family. It was imperative that today's youngsters keep their eyes wide open.

Zoe's parents hadn't tried to shield her from reality, only from peril. Ione and Rupert Strasse had brought their daughter along to Greece. Until Alec Westerlin's shocking death, they had treated her as a full-fledged member of their team. Then, hoping to protect her, they'd sent her home. And now for everyone's safety it was vital that she stay alert.

The moment's respite had given Kelsey a

chance to regain her self-confidence. In a quiet tone she gave a simple but truthful account of what had precipitated their headlong flight.

A look of relief spread over Zoe's small face as soon as she realized that no deep, dark secrets were being kept from her. 'That man in the rattly green car? I saw him too.'

Kelsey glanced over at the massive doors. No one had made any attempt to follow them inside. Her imagination might just have been working overtime. 'Seeing him twice was an upsetting coincidence, but that doesn't prove he meant us any harm. I acted on impulse instead of stopping to weigh the possibilities.'

Zoe looped her arms affectionately around Kelsey's neck. 'The night Uncle Michael went away, he told me he was a real good judge of people. He said he would trust you with his life and that I should too. That I could count on you to see me through, no matter what.'

Lucky thing Uncle Michael hadn't been around ten minutes earlier, Kelsey thought wryly. Even so, she felt tears smart at the edges of her tired eyes. 'That was nice of him to say, considering we didn't have very long to get acquainted.'

'Oh, he'd already found out a whole lot about you from Joanna,' Zoe confided with an innocent smile. 'He told me if you said "run," I should skedaddle and that I was to help you all I could.' She slid out of the chair and turned toward the door. 'Want me to look outside and see if that man is still there?'

'Thanks, honey, but I don't think that would be a good idea.' As Kelsey, too, stood up, she noticed that a middle-aged man in a business suit had appeared from the rear premises to hover behind the registration desk. Undoubtedly, he wished she would hurry and state her business so he could get back to his afternoon siesta. Her voice dropped to a whisper as she bent close to Zoe on the pretext of gathering up their luggage. 'Once the desk clerk finds out that we're staying here at the hotel, he can keep an eye out for strangers on our behalf. But while we talk to him, or to anyone else from now on, remember who you are.'

'Uh-huh. Jason.'

'That's right. And Jason is a very shy boy, isn't he?'

Zoe ducked her head and stuck her thumb in her mouth.

In spite of how worried she'd been only moments before, Kelsey found herself laughing. 'Perfect! A little mouse couldn't look more timid. Okay, here we go.'

While Zoe trailed along, clutching her skirt, Kelsey crossed the room and gave the man behind the desk a pleasant smile. 'Hello. Reservations were made for us by a relative,' she said, feeling it was unnecessary to add that Michael Devos was Zoe's relative, not hers. 'The name is Anderson.'

'Welcome to the Acantha, *Kyria* Anderson!' Smiling widely now, he handed her a registration card to fill out. A double for herself and the little one was all prepared, he assured her. Then he looked across at the chair where she and Zoe had sat for a moment, and gave way to his curiosity. 'You were not feeling ill, I hope?'

'No...'

Kelsey let her voice trail off while considering the best way to ensure their security here at the hotel. Greece, from all she had heard and read, was still very much a man's country. While women were cherished, they were also usually expected to stay at home and care for the house and children. Suspecting that the average male's machismo would cause him to immediately spring to the defense of a 'helpless' female, she decided to make use of this traditional attitude for the sake of Zoe's protection.

'No,' she repeated, 'I wasn't ill, just upset. At the airport a man kept staring at me.'

'The *kyria's* so-beautiful hair caught his attention, understandably.'

Judging from the admiration in his round black eyes, the flowery compliment was meant sincerely. For the first time in her life Kelsey almost regretted not having been born a petite charmer. Independent young career women who towered over half the men of their acquaintance didn't get much practice at fluttering their eyelashes.

She did her best to look as though she were counting on him to be her big, strong protector. 'How kind of you to say so, *kyrie*. I would not have been so distressed except that he trailed along after our bus and pulled up right across the street. I was never so happy to see anything as the sign for your hotel!'

The hotel manager's face grew stern. Anyone would have thought a member of his own family had been insulted. 'You say this scoundrel followed you *here*?'

There was no need for Kelsey to sham apprehension when she remembered how she'd been pinpointed by the man's narrowed eyes through the window of the bus. 'Yes. When we ran inside, he was just getting out of his car. It was green—an old Renault, I think.'

'Have no fear, *Kyria* Anderson. If he is still outside, he will soon hear a few sharp words from Spyridon Poulous!'

Stalking out from behind the desk, he marched across the lobby. Almost the instant he tugged the door open, his indignation was replaced by amusement. 'I believe the man you mentioned has already received his comeuppance. He had the misfortune to suffer a puncture in the space reserved for buses to stop. Even now a policeman is writing up a summons. Without a doubt the tow truck is on its way.'

It was clear that the manager believed it was

the flat tire rather than a dogged pursuit of Kelsey that had caused the driver of the green Renault to pull up to the curb across the street. Praying that he was right, she brought up the subject of food.

'The dinner hour here in Athens is very late, I've heard. I'm afraid we've missed a couple of meals during our journey. Could you recommend a place where we could get a little something to eat, once we've had a chance to wash and rest?'

'But of course. The Acantha has its own roof-garden restaurant,' he proudly declared. 'So wonderful a view you would not believe. You must see it for yourself. Naturally, as you say, the full dinner is not available until ten o'clock. But after five, when our siesta period comes to an end, the waiter will be happy to serve you and the little one a light meal.'

Their room was located on the shady side of the building, a definite plus, since the Acantha's amenities apparently did not include air-conditioning. Kelsey tipped the teenage bellhop with a dollar's worth of drachmas and was thanked by a beaming smile and a voluble flood of Greek.

'He said you were generous and good, besides being as beautiful as Athena herself,' Zoe translated with a giggle the moment the door closed behind him.

Kelsey began to understand why Greece was such a popular vacation destination for

Scandinavian women. Just then, however, the sight of comfortable twin beds and the spotlessly clean tub in the adjoining bathroom was more welcome than the most lavish of compliments.

She was rinsing shampoo out of Zoe's hair and looking forward to her own bath when the bellboy returned to knock on the door and announce that a telephone call had come for the *kyria*. The wall-mounted instrument out in the corridor was evidently meant to serve the needs of all third-floor tenants. Kelsey stepped out, warily turning the key in the lock before picking up the receiver.

'*Embros*,' she tried out one of her newly acquired words of Greek. 'Who is calling, please?'

'A friend who is happy you've arrived safely,' responded a reassuring male voice. 'Did you have a pleasant trip?'

Michael! Kelsey smiled as she pictured the man on the other end of the line. 'Smooth as silk,' she replied. 'The one disappointment was not having you there to meet us on arrival.'

'You weren't half so disappointed about that as I was,' Michael declared. 'When I spoke with your cousin, I'd had every intention of being on the spot when your plane landed. Then at the last minute I picked up some important information. I felt it was essential to check it out immediately.'

'This has to do with your relatives?'

Approval of her discretion warmed his voice. 'Yes. The timing couldn't be worse, but this lead was too promising to ignore. I promise it will take only a day and a half at most to learn if it's true or just another red herring.'

From this Kelsey assumed that his investigation had so far led to nothing but blind alleys. While she sympathized, his continued absence left her with a dilemma. 'I understand, of course. While you're away, would it be all right if we went out and got acquainted with Athens? Both of us nearly developed cabin fever after a solid week in the house at home.'

The barest of pauses preceded Michael's reply. 'Sure,' he said. 'You've been a trouper about taking on this job without a bit of fuss. Just don't go too far from the hotel, okay? No running off to Delphi to consult the Oracle, or anything like that. Later you'll have a chance to see everything.'

Seeing everything all by herself didn't sound like a whole lot of fun, Kelsey ruminated perversely. Still, she was here to do a job, not to take a vacation. Besides, it was the classical sites right here in the old part of Athens that she was most eager to visit.

'That suits me fine,' she agreed. 'There was one unsettling incident I think you should know about—'

A sonorous rumble, part of the background

noise on the other end of the line, interrupted her attempt to tell him about the man in the green Renault. Michael broke in with a hasty good-bye. 'Gotta run, or I'll miss the ferry. I sent word to a friend to stay close in case you need an ally. Love to you-know-who. See you both day after tomorrow.'

Kelsey hung up, swallowing a sigh of frustration. While it was nice to know she had an ally, she wished Michael could have spared the time to identify this mysterious friend he had spoken of. And to listen to one other piece of news as well. It was going to be interesting to see the look on his face when he realized that 'you-know-who' was currently masquerading as a nephew rather than a niece.

Moments later, sliding into a tub of warm, foamy water, she was still thinking of Michael. His mention of a ferryboat left no doubt in her mind that he was headed for an island. Not that that conclusion did much to narrow down his destination. According to legend, when God was finished creating the Earth, there were a handful of rocks left over. Scooping them up, He tossed them over His mighty shoulder—and they became the islands of Greece. There were one thousand, four hundred and twenty-five of them, if her guidebook was to be believed, although less than two hundred were actually inhabited. How many, she wondered, lay along the route of the ferryboats?

A nine-hour time difference existed between Greece and the West Coast of North America. Stretching out on her bed, Kelsey gave thanks for the custom of siesta in hot countries. Maybe a nap would help her system begin to adjusting to the climate—as well as to eating breakfast at her regular dinnertime. Because of the fierce midday heat, stores and offices opened early, then closed down tight between one-thirty and five every afternoon. Some of them reopened for several hours in the evening. No wonder, she decided, drifting off to sleep, that the Greek dinner hour started so late!

When she awoke, it was after six, and the room seemed a trifle cooler. Her eyes felt less gritty, too, after the sound sleep. And she was starved! She'd eaten very little during the journey, in the hope of counteracting jet lag; now her system was agitating for food. Hopping up, she put on a lightweight skirt and blouse and was thrusting her toes into low-heeled shoes when Zoe rolled over in her own bed and yawned.

'Awake, pumpkin?' Kelsey unearthed a set of cool seersucker play clothes from the knapsack and handed the child a pair of tiny red sandals. 'As soon as you're dressed, we'll go track down something to eat. After that, if we feel like it, we can come back to bed. By morning I hope we'll be rested up enough to do some sight-seeing.'

But when they emerged onto the picturesque

67

rooftop setting where the restaurant was located, Kelsey wondered how she could manage to wait that long. As the hotel manager had guaranteed, the scene that met her eyes was absolutely breathtaking. From their table she had an unimpeded view of a large white cliff in the near distance, rising a couple of hundred feet above the rooftops. The sun had begun to sink toward the horizon, and golden light flooded the vista, illuminating every column, every soaring marbled structure, as if indeed some benevolent immortal were looking down with favor on this very special place.

'My mom told me the Acropolis is called the Sacred Rock,' Zoe said, noticing the rapt expression on Kelsey's face.

'Oh, it's magnificent!'

Framed by an impressive backdrop of mountains, the Acropolis was the focal point of the entire Plain of Attica, as the flat valley on which Athens stood was called. Surely, she thought, their designers must have positioned those fabulous structures crowning the heights so that each of them could be seen and appreciated by the ordinary people of the town as they went about their day's work. The Athenians in this ancient neighborhood were still fortunate in that respect. All around the hotel were other two- and three-story buildings, each with its own rooftop garden where people could sit out and enjoy the view.

The Parthenon, a beautiful Doric temple, was the crowning glory of the Acropolis. It had been built in honor of Athena, the patron goddess of the city of Athens, and was a classic example of grace in architecture. Kelsey had read that there was not a straight line in the entire design. The timeless structure had remained almost completely unchanged for very close to two thousand years before being damaged in a war between the Turks and the Venetians.

Yet even now, in this light, it appeared perfect. A dazzling sight to behold. Were Michael Devos to show up on Wednesday with Zoe's parents in tow and a thank-you for her time and trouble in looking after his niece, Kelsey would have felt amply rewarded. Just being here—seeing this—was the experience of a lifetime.

A waiter approached, asked their pleasure, and went away again. In time he returned with bowls of thick soup enriched by chunks of lamb and pasta, tomatoes and other tender vegetables. There was salad as well, glossy black olives, and cubes of pale white feta cheese, made from goats' milk, nestled among succulent greens and glistening with a dressing of olive oil. A basket of rolls accompanied this hearty fare, and tall glasses of icy, fresh-squeezed lemonade.

When every tasty morsel had disappeared, Kelsey ordered more lemonade for Zoe and coffee for herself to accompany dessert. The squares of baklava were incredibly sweet, made from countless layers of phyllo dough, and dripping with honey and chopped nuts. After setting finger bowls in front of them, the young waiter, whose English was good, lingered companionably, since they were among the very few patrons yet to arrive.

In the past, he informed them, he had worked aboard a cruise ship. At Kelsey's encouragement he told them a little about the area where they were staying.

In 1834, when it achieved its independence and became the capital of modern Greece after five centuries of Turkish rule, only about five thousand people lived in Athens. All of them were crowded into the old quarter. Since then the city had sprawled out in all directions. Now it was home to more than three million people.

'You must go to see our Royal Palace, *kyria*, and the Parliament buildings on the other side of Constitution Square,' he urged.

'We're looking forward to it.' A discreet inspection of their bill showed that the reasonable sum already included a fifteen percent surcharge for service. Even so, Kelsey added a small token tip to the money she placed on the tray. This was her way of showing she appreciated his pleasant attitude, as well as his sincere concern that they see everything his city had to offer. 'For the first day or two, though, I think there's enough to keep us fascinated right here in the old quarter. *Kalispera*,' she added, trying out what she hoped was the correct phrase as they turned to leave the rooftop restaurant. 'Good night.'

* * *

Even before eight in the morning, the glare was formidable. At the hotel they'd been given directions on where to catch the bus that would take them to the gateway of the Acropolis. Glad that she'd had the good sense to bring along dark glasses and shady straw hats for them both, Kelsey took Zoe's hand for the trudge the rest of the way up the steep incline.

At the top she could see that the ancient temples had suffered many blemishes over time that weren't noticeable from a distance. Broken columns had been left to lay where they fell, and the footing as they approached the Parthenon was anything but level.

They were not the only sightseers who had decided to make an early start. Guides were shepherding numerous small groups of tourists along, pausing for frequent mini-lectures as they moved from spot to spot. Kelsey heard French and Italian spoken, and the staccato syllables of Japanese. Then, to her delighted surprise, her ears picked up a voice describing the Temple of the Winged Victory in Norwegian.

As children, she and Joanna and their

brothers had learned this language from their great-grandparents, who had come to America from Oslo. Among the family they still often spoke Norse at home. Now, remembering Michael's advice that she and Zoe mingle with the many Scandinavians visiting Greece, she unobtrusively attached herself and Zoe to this group.

Her small charge looked puzzled. 'What's he saying?'

'All Greek to you, huh?' Kelsey joked and interpreted the gist of the guide's words. 'He's telling the people that the golden marble used to build all these marvelous temples was taken from that mountain up there, the one called Pendeli. When they were all in place, the columns and pediments were painted in bright colors. It sounds strange because that isn't what we're used to seeing, but the people who lived here then liked it that way. Over the centuries the paint wore away, leaving just the stone itself behind.'

Trailing along for a close look at a temple known as the Erechtheion, Kelsey heard the guide complain that one of the caryatids, or statues of women that were used as columns, was a modern-day replacement. Along with many sculptures from the Parthenon and other places, the original had been removed in the early 1800s. At that time the Greeks had not yet won their freedom from Turkey. Lord Elgin, the British Ambassador to

Constantinople—now called Istanbul—received permission from the Turkish government to take away a number of priceless marble carvings from the Acropolis and other historic spots in Greece. He had them shipped off to London, then sold them to the British Museum.

Rather like Heinrich Schliemann digging up Troy and hauling all the wonderful objects he found there off to Berlin, Kelsey thought. Nowadays that would never be allowed to happen.

'Our government is still clamoring for the return of these treasures that are known as the Elgin Marbles,' the guide added indignantly.

Michael had mentioned that heavy penalties were imposed on anyone attempting to remove so much as a chip of marble from Greece. Hearing the guide's aggrieved remarks, Kelsey could understand why. She had noticed a number of stalwart young men clad in striking native costumes posted in various spots around the Acropolis, making sure that the ancient ruins were treated with respect. Zoe said these guards were called *Evzones*. They were an elite group who also watched over the Royal Palace and other important places in Greece.

The heat of the day was building up rapidly, and Zoe's short legs were finding all this trudging around rough going. Kelsey took her hand. Together, they moved away from the

73

group, into the shade. Walking slowly, they found their way down to the first of a spectacular pair of open-air theaters. It was connected with the second outdoor auditorium by way of a *stoa*, or covered walkway, that had undergone some impressive restoration.

With tired sighs they sank down in seats at the top row of the Odeon of Herodes Atticus. What a pleasure, Kelsey reflected, simply to sit and absorb the view! Tall, slender cypress trees added touches of greenery to the pale houses and winding streets spread out far below. From this height it was easy to remember that Socrates and Plato and Aristotle—all those early teachers and scholars who had contributed so much to the world's knowledge—might still be down there in the old-time marketplace that was called the Agora, going about their business.

'Mom and Dad and I were s'posed to come see a play here.' Zoe's tone was mournful. 'We planned to spend a whole week in Athens, doing all sorts of interesting stuff. But instead, I had to go home.'

Kelsey gave her a comforting hug. She knew the little girl was very worried about her parents. Talking about missing a performance of *Electra* wasn't so disheartening as having to admit that the people she loved best in the whole world had dropped out of sight and that nobody had any idea of what could have happened to them.

'They wanted to make sure you stayed safe,' she said consolingly. 'When I talked with your Uncle Michael on the phone yesterday, he was on his way to check out a promising bit of information that he hoped would lead to them.'

'Yes, you told me. But, Kelsey, I don't think he can do it without those special maps my mom drew. There was something particular 'bout them that I've been trying to remember. The islands looked different from the ones you and I saw in the atlas.'

Islands? With a sinking heart Kelsey remembered the ferryboat's loud toot cutting short her conversation with Michael. She didn't understand what Zoe was getting at. The little girl didn't seem to be sure herself. But if there was anything to this notion of a different set of islands, it sounded as if Michael might be off on yet another wild-goose chase.

Maps were maps, though—weren't they? Nowadays cartography was an exact science.

Still, she remembered, Ione Devos Strasse was a classical scholar. Her drawings might be based on landmarks that hadn't been around recently. Say, in the past two thousand years or so.

'What do you mean, honey—"different"?'

Zoe puckered up her forehead. Even though she squeezed her eyes shut, she wasn't able to be much more specific. 'Just different,' she said with a catch in her voice. 'Crowdeder together down in the corner.'

Kelsey tried hard not to show her concern. 'Crowdeder together' wasn't apt to go very far in helping them locate Ione and Rupert. But Zoe was tired now, hot and fretful. Tomorrow when she was in better spirits, Michael would probably have better luck encouraging her to be specific.

Standing up, she took the child's hand and headed back toward the exit from the Sacred Rock. Lunch might help, and a siesta.

The truth of the matter was, she was a little afraid to think about tomorrow. Not just because Michael hadn't had time to tell her how and where they were supposed to meet. Those were details that could easily be worked out. No, tomorrow was a bugaboo because there was a chance that when he returned from wherever he'd been, he would have learned that something terrible had happened to his sister and her husband.

Kelsey looked down at the trusting little girl walking downhill beside her and ordered herself to stop dredging up pessimistic possibilities. Either this rumor Michael was chasing would have led him to Ione and Rupert, or it would prove to be a total washout. In that case no news was good news. If he had been looking for them in all the wrong places, the search would just have to go on until the right place turned up.

And in the meantime...

Her heart beat a little faster. In the meantime she'd be seeing him again.

CHAPTER FIVE

The Intruder is on the flight deck...
Kelsey's breath jammed in her throat. For the past thirty-six hours she had done her level best to avoid thinking about Michael Devos. This morning, walking back to their room with Zoe after breakfast, her mind had been busy with other matters. But the moment she unfolded the note that had been shoved underneath the door during their absence, her heart gave a giant leap. He had promised to join them on Wednesday.

Today!

She had seen this identical handwriting ten days ago, on a list of names and addresses Michael handed her before leaving Seattle. 'If I should happen to disappear in Greece, any of these people will gladly take responsibility for my niece,' he'd stated. 'Whatever happens, you won't need to worry about looking after her indefinitely.'

His no-nonsense attitude checked the protest that rose to Kelsey's lips. Reminding herself that he had good reason to plan ahead for all eventualities, she had tucked the list away for safekeeping. Now, unexpectedly, here was the same penmanship again, dashed across a sheet of ordinary lined paper.

Even if she'd had the least doubt about the writer's identity, the message began with the password they had agreed to use.

Thankful that Zoe had marched straight on into the bathroom, Kelsey locked the door to the corridor, then leaned against it, crossing her fingers, gathering courage to read further. With all her heart she prayed that this communication from Michael would declare that their worries were over, that his sister and brother-in-law had turned up, safe and sound.

To her disappointment, no mention at all was made of Ione and Rupert. Instead, the paper in her hand contained a concise set of instructions. After the maid had finished tidying the room later that morning, Michael directed, Kelsey was to pack up all their belongings and stack the luggage against the wall, just inside the door. Somebody else would collect it a and take care of checking them out of the hotel. By then they would already have departed.

Departed for where? she wondered in distraction. Hadn't she and Zoe already flown through nine time zones, more than a third of the way around the world? Where were they expected to head off to next?

The firm handwriting clarified that point. A central departure zone for sight-seeing buses was located on Adrianou Street, three blocks north of the hotel. Prepaid tickets were being held for them at the kiosk there. The tourist policeman in charge of the booth would hand them over on request and point out the bus scheduled to leave for Daphni at one o'clock.

As she turned the sheet of paper over, Kelsey anticipated some mention of Michael's own plans. Would he meet them on the tour bus? At Daphni, wherever that was? But the reverse side of the page was blank. They were operating strictly on a 'need to know' basis here, apparently.

Muffling a sigh, she told herself that she had no choice except to follow directions and trust that everything would work out all right. It had been that way from the very beginning. So far Michael hadn't let them down. Back in Seattle he'd filled her in on the background and leveled with her about the potential danger. But it would have been helpful if he'd been a little more forthcoming now, instead of asking her to go on playing blindman's buff in a situation where one slip could mean disaster.

Still, he knew that even better than she, Kelsey conceded. These elaborate precautions were meant to keep them all safe. Zoe in particular. As for herself, she'd agreed to do her part. Complaints about being kept in the dark hadn't been part of the deal.

She folded Michael's note, tucked it away in her deep skirt pocket, and reached for the soft-cover guidebook she'd been relying on for information about Greece. Perhaps it could tell her what to expect from this place they were slated to see this afternoon.

By the time Zoe plopped down on the bed beside her, Kelsey had gathered a few facts. Daphni was described as being an interesting locale a few miles outside of Athens. An eleventh-century Byzantine church shared the site with a monastery predating it by seven hundred years. The materials used to construct that building and its battlemented walls had been taken from the ancient Sanctuary of Apollo, which had occupied the site much earlier.

'It's still hard to believe how old so many things are around here,' Kelsey said to the little girl beside her. Washington, where she lived, had just celebrated its centennial. One hundred years of statehood had seemed like quite a long stretch of time. But here in Greece buildings sometimes endured for two or three *thousand* years, and nobody seemed to consider that particularly unusual.

Michael's brusque instructions had given her no idea of what to expect once they were aboard the bus and headed for Daphni. Since another person had been assigned the task of collecting their luggage and checking them out of the hotel, she suspected that they wouldn't be coming back to Athens. Not right away, at least. An ache hung like lead in her chest. There was so much left to see. All those awe-inspiring links with the past she had hoped to study and learn from. Now there might never be an opportunity.

Kelsey told herself to stop being a nitwit. Precious minutes were flying by while she sat here feeling sorry for herself. Michael's instructions had been quite specific. She was *not* to pack until the maid had been in to make the beds, presumably to keep from tipping off anyone about their impending departure. That left hours yet to roam about the *Plaka*, to store up all sorts of wonders in her memory.

'Got your comfortable walking shoes on?' she asked Zoe. 'Let's go hit the cobblestones and visit Hadrian's Arch.'

Other tourists besides themselves were strolling about the oldest quarter of the city, absorbing the sights and sounds and smells of Greece. Once again Kelsey marveled at the intensity of the light flooding down out of the cloudless blue sky. In spite of their great age, the whitewashed houses and twisting alleyways were limned with a radiance she'd never seen elsewhere.

With its water clock and sundial, the ancient Tower of the Winds was fascinating. Waiting until nobody else was around, Zoe translated the inscription at the monument of Lysicrates. It had been erected to honor a victory in a musical contest, she said. Though she enjoyed the morning, Kelsey was edgily aware of time spinning away. After glimpsing the house

81

where the English poet Lord Byron had lived while writing one of his most famous poems, she turned back toward the Acantha.

As expected, Zoe eagerly asked for news of her parents the instant she learned that Michael had been in touch. Kelsey would have given anything to have some heartening tidings to report. 'Your uncle's too cautious to say more in a note than he really needed to,' she reminded the little girl, then stemmed the flood of questions by providing work for idle hands. 'Let's get packed. Haul your pajamas and slippers out of the closet so we can squash them into your knapsack.'

'Squash' was the word, all right. Even though she hadn't added a thing, her own suitcase closed with difficulty too. Kelsey wondered how Sarah Twelvetrees managed to make room for all the things she must acquire during those shopping binges of hers. Probably by carrying extra pieces of luggage wherever she went.

Kelsey forgot her problems with the bulging baggage when she saw Zoe walk past the dressing-table mirror, and pause to stick her tongue out.

'I'll sure be glad when nobody's looking for me anymore,' the small, mournful voice declared. 'I thought that playing Jason would be an exciting adventure, but it hasn't been any fun at all. Do you s'pose Uncle Michael will laugh at the way I look?'

82

'Of course not. He'll compliment you for having thought up such a clever disguise.'

Poor kid. It must have been even more difficult than she'd realized for the bright, chatty youngster to masquerade as a tongue-tied little boy, Kelsey thought with a pang. The mythical Jason might have sailed happily off to lead the Argonauts in their quest for the Golden Fleece, but his modern-day namesake just wanted to find her missing family and go home.

'Besides,' she added, beginning to plait her own long, fair hair into braids that could be wound around her head for coolness, 'Jason's haircut is lots more practical than a ponytail in this sizzling climate. Did you check under the bed to make sure nothing's been left behind?'

*　　　*　　　*

The pickup point for the escorted tours was easily located. Kelsey was relieved to spot a tiny Union Jack among the cluster of flags displayed on the policeman's tunic pocket, proclaiming the fact that he spoke English in addition to several other languages. Moments later, thanks to his efficiency, she and Zoe were climbing aboard one of the big diesel rigs. Moving down the aisle toward a pair of unoccupied rear seats, she gazed hopefully at each of their fellow passengers. Nobody looked the least bit familiar.

She hadn't really expected Michael to be aboard, waiting for them, Kelsey acknowledged. Otherwise what would have been the point of all this cloak-and-dagger subterfuge? Slipping casually out of the hotel, pretending enthusiasm for a tour of an ancient site she'd never heard of until this morning, keeping Zoe close at all times—

Fear, sharp and numbing, ripped through her consciousness as a vivid flash of green whipped past, speeding in the opposite direction. She swiveled around, mashing her face against the pane of glass, but the car was already out of sight. There was no way to make certain it was the same battered vehicle that had trailed them into the city from the airport the day of their arrival.

Even if it had been, she thought, trying to calm herself as she settled back in the seat, the driver obviously had no interest in the people aboard this bus. All she had to do was relax. Let herself be conveyed to Daphni. And Michael—she hoped. Feeling her way in the dark was beginning to make her very nervous. She wondered how spies kept from getting ulcers.

As soon as they'd cleared the worst of the traffic, the tour guide clicked on her microphone. Speaking first in French, then in English, she told the passengers that *daphni* was a Greek word meaning laurel trees. Laurels had once grown thickly all about the

84

place they were to visit.

'Wreaths were made from the branches and leaves of these trees to crown the winners in sporting events,' she went on. 'Later in the summer, wine festivals will be held at Daphni. But before the grapes are harvested, the grounds are used as campsites. People wanting to get away from the city for a few days come here with their tents and bedrolls to enjoy the open air.'

Was that what Michael was doing? Kelsey wondered. Losing himself among throngs of campers and backpackers? It seemed unlikely. For the past few days, at least, he'd been away, chasing down a rumor out in the Aegean somewhere, on one of the islands.

That cluster of islands Zoe had insisted looked different from those pictured in the atlas, she remembered. That statement still puzzled her. But if Michael's search for Ione and Rupert had proved successful, they wouldn't need to worry about the riddle any longer.

Minutes away from their destination, Kelsey was listening to the tour guide describe the Sanctuary of Apollo when she saw the car again. This time, as it swooped past the bus on the left, there was no doubt at all about its make. As it roared down the dusty road and vanished from sight, she reminded herself that there must be thousands of the economical little French cars here in Athens. She had heard that in Europe the cost of gasoline was sky high; according to the remarks of an Australian couple across the aisle, fuel was even more expensive here in Greece than in other parts of the Continent.

No wonder there were so many motor scooters all over the city. Motor scooters and green Renaults...

Soon afterward, the driver braked and pulled in to park beside another tour bus. Stepping out first, the guide cautioned the group that they would be returning to the city promptly at five o'clock. 'This way, please,' she ordered briskly. 'Daphni has much of interest to see. The mosaics in the Byzantine chapel are particularly fine...'

Kelsey and Zoe had been seated near the rear of the bus. By the time they stepped out onto the grass, all but a few members of the tour party were hastening in the direction of the domed church, a large stone structure roofed in tile. Kelsey couldn't blame them. The outdoors heat was intense. Yet she hesitated, uncertain as to how to proceed, while the remaining passengers surged past to catch up with the main group.

Here they were, she thought, in beautiful downtown Daphni. What would Michael want them to do now? Stick with the rest of the tour? Or—

Movement from the side caught her eye. Kelsey grabbed Zoe's hand and gripped it tightly, weighing her options as the short man she had first noticed outside Hellikon Airport moved steadily toward them. Already the driver had locked the bus and ambled off, intent, no doubt, on a siesta under a shade tree until he was needed for the return trip to the city. There was no hope of hopping back aboard and slamming the door. And making a run for the now-distant group, as she had run for the Acantha days earlier, seemed like a stopgap measure, at best.

There were plenty of people in the vicinity in case she decided to scream for help. But resentment at having her heels dogged prompted her to choose a different course. The best defense, she had always heard, was a good offense. Who did this nuisance of a man think he was, anyway, tagging after them all over Greece?

Kelsey took a determined step toward him, noticing that he was neither young nor particularly burly. He might have been anywhere between forty and sixty-five.

'What do you want?' she demanded. 'Go away! Stop bothering us, or I'll call a policeman.'

His black eyes widened a bit at her stern challenge, but he did not seem particularly intimidated. '*Ne, ne,*' he said, nodding. 'Police is good. But not needed. Come you, this way.'

'No, *you* go that way. And make it fast!'

The man, a Greek, didn't seem able to speak

English very well. Kelsey had half a notion to have Zoe repeat the order in the vernacular, just to make sure he got the message. Instinct warned against such a move, urging her to keep the little girl as far out of the picture as possible. She could handle this confrontation herself. She had to!

The too-familiar stranger had halted six feet away. He seemed surprised by her refusal to follow his orders. The fact that she stood there glowering at him instead of trotting obediently along like any of the docile females of his acquaintance was clearly not what he had expected.

'*Parakalo, thespinas*,' he protested. 'Please, Miss—'

Struggling with a language barrier of her own, Kelsey wasn't able to make a bit of sense out of the rest of what he said. Yet rather than being reassured by the two words she *had* understood, they'd left her feeling more wary than ever. He had called her 'Miss.' *Why?* she wondered suspiciously. Everyone else just automatically addressed her as *kyria*—Mrs—going on the assumption that a female with a young child in tow must be a married woman and the little one's mother.

How had this man come by his assurance that that wasn't the case at all?

Zoe tugged urgently at her hand, whispering a translation into Kelsey's ear as she bent down. 'He says his name is Yannis Papadakis.

A friend wants him to bring us to him. It isn't far to go. Just around to the other side of that big wall. Yannis says not to be afraid. He's strong and trustworthy, and he'll guard us with his life.'

Uh-huh. And if she believed that, he probably had a bridge he'd be glad to sell her, Kelsey thought scornfully. Or maybe a nice Doric temple up on a cliff somewhere.

Yet it was hard to reject that sincere expression of his.

Since Zoe's command of Greek was no longer a secret, she decided to use the youngster to find out what they needed to know. But the request she whispered contained a subtle warning, reminding the child to stay in character.

'Ask him who this friend is, Jason. And find out if there was something special he was supposed to say to us.'

Almost the instant the second question was rattled off in his own language, Yannis Papadakis made a thumping gesture against his forehead with the heel of his hand. It was one of those universal motions that seemed to say, 'How could I have been so absent-minded?'

Before answering, he scanned the vicinity through his perpetually narrowed eyes, making certain no one else was in earshot. Then he spoke a name, one that Kelsey had no difficulty in recognizing. Except for one word, the next sentence didn't translate. She had a reasonably good hunch, however, as to what he'd said.

The name was Michael Devos. And the word, that one significant word, was *Intruder*.

Kelsey thought hard. A lot was riding on what she did next. Whether or not she decided to believe him. Was it possible Yannis could be trustworthy? On the phone Michael had told her he'd sent word to a friend to stay close in trouble. Once or twice since then it had crossed her mind to wonder whether he could have meant Sarah Twelvetrees. That made little sense, though. Their seatmate from the London flight had hurried away as soon as the plane set down in Athens.

Still, never in a million years would it have occurred to her that this rather intimidating little man who went dashing around in a beat-up old green car might have been assigned to act as their guardian angel. In fact, she'd been all but convinced that he must be working for Michael's enemies.

And that might very well be, she cautioned herself. Whatever side he was on, he'd evidently been keeping an eye on them since their arrival. He could have managed to get a prying glimpse of the note that had been pushed underneath their door this morning. One quick look would have been enough to intercept that coded phrase.

Rigid with apprehension, Kelsey twined her fingers through Zoe's and murmured a set of low-voiced instructions. 'Don't say anything about your uncle. Just ask this man which Intruder he's talking about. Be ready to run. We'll make a dash toward that sidewalk café over there if I don't like the sound of the answer he gives.'

But to her intense relief that turned out to be unnecessary. Yannis Papadakis looked straight at Kelsey. 'The F-14,' he said clearly. Unmistakably.

She gave the small hand in hers a reassuring squeeze. It was all right! Only a real friend would have known what to say!

As she straightened up, Kelsey motioned for Yannis to lead the way. The three of them hurried across the meadow toward the wall he'd pointed out. It was undoubtedly the one her guidebook had called 'battlemented,' with crenels or squarish slots on the top for defenders to shoot through in times of siege. How odd that they'd taken once-hallowed stone from Apollo's ancient sanctuary.

But suddenly she didn't care how or why it had been erected. Because waiting behind that wall, with a look of glad welcome on his face, was Michael Devos.

Zoe took one look at her uncle and rocketed into his waiting arms. Kelsey found herself longing to follow suit. Sternly resisting the impulse, she lagged behind until Michael held out his hand to draw her near. 'You have no idea how delighted I am to see you both,' he

91

said, so earnestly that Kelsey felt a stirring in her heart. 'A couple of times recently I wasn't so sure—'

If he added anything else, she didn't take it in. Suddenly she'd caught sight of the white slash of bandage across his temple. For a second or two her stricken gaze locked with his. Then Michael's dark eyes slid sideways to the little girl in his arms. His head gave an almost imperceptible shake.

Whatever was going on, Kelsey realized at once, he didn't want it discussed in front of Zoe. Nodding, she drew her fingers out of his strong, warm grip. *First things first*, she told herself, trying not to dwell on what might have happened to injure him.

She watched him turn with thanks to the other man. '*Efharisto*, Yannis, for all your help. I knew I could count on my father's boyhood friend.'

The slitted eyes looked suspiciously bright as Yannis clapped the younger man on the shoulder. He said something in Greek. *Farewell*, Kelsey thought, interpreting the tone rather than the words. *And be careful!* Then he was gone, and the three of them were hurrying toward a compact gray car parked along the roadside.

Michael ruffled Zoe's cropped hair while holding the door open for them to pile in. 'What happened here? Stand too close to a lawnmower?'

Knowing how eager the youngster was to bombard him with questions about her parents, Kelsey guessed that the joke had been calculated to make her laugh and take her mind off more serious matters. So he hadn't found Ione and Rupert, she thought, and forced a smile at Zoe's quick comeback.

'Uncle Michael! Can't you tell I'm in disguise? When other people are around, you're s'posed to call me Jason.'

'You have my word on it, Zoe/Jason. I always knew you were a smart cookie.' He hurried around to the driver's seat and glanced over at Kelsey as he started the engine. 'Keeping the luggage down to a minimum was an intelligent move too. Having only the two pieces to handle made it easier for Yannis to cope at the hotel. I'd have felt rotten asking him to wrestle with the half dozen suitcases some people would have dragged along.'

Kelsey had already spotted their bags on the back-seat. Today's arrangements, at least, seemed to have gone off like clockwork. Something terribly unforeseen must have happened on that ferryboat trip, though.

There would have been little chance to ask questions even had the wide-eyed youngster not been seated between them. Michael drove fast, guiding the car expertly past slower traffic. His attention seemed almost equally divided between the road in front of him and the ribbon of pavement visible in the rearview mirror.

Minutes after passing through the outskirts of an industrial-looking town called Eleusis, Kelsey caught sight of the sea sparkling ahead. So far as she was able to tell, they had not been followed. Then when Michael turned onto a graveled stretch leading down to the water, she realized that even if they had picked up a tail, it wouldn't matter for long. A small seaplane, painted pale blue and white to match the colors in the Greek flag, had just landed and was taxiing toward them through the shallows.

'Perfect timing, *ne?*'

The exuberant young pilot who swung down from the cockpit was called Dion. He seemed quite content to trade his plane temporarily for the ground transportation in which they had arrived. His teeth looked very white against his olive skin as he flashed Kelsey an engaging grin and invited her to come along and keep him company.

'Sorry, cousin. Find your own girl.' Imperturbably Michael boosted his companions into the amphibian and handed their luggage up for them to stow. While they were fastening their seat belts, he turned back for a quick exchange with the other pilot. 'Everything's all set?'

Dion nodded. 'Stefanos will be fishing about a mile offshore. Set her down and trade places with him. The boat is yours for as long as you need it.'

They took off with a controlled surge of power. Once they had leveled off and she could make herself heard again, Kelsey laughed and shook her head. 'We seem to be playing a game of musical chairs!'

Michael didn't laugh back. 'It's no game.'

Her smile faded. 'No. Of course it isn't.' She hoped he didn't think she was taking all this too lightly. 'Is Dion really your cousin?'

'Yes, but so distant we'd need the family Bible to trace the links. And Stefanos, whom you'll meet in an hour, is Yannis's grandson.' Michael scowled into the distance. 'I'm counting on our adversary underestimating the strength of blood and cultural ties. With Greeks, loyalty to family and friends is basic. As natural as breathing. A matter of honor.'

'Like refusing to let the language die out?' That night in Seattle he had told her that during the five hundred years of the Turkish occupation, Greek was banned from the schools. People were forbidden to use it in public. Quietly, families spoke it at home and even more quietly taught their children. The day the Turks left, the entire country went back to speaking its own language again. It seemed like an awesome achievement to Kelsey, though the Greeks apparently considered it quite unremarkable. They were not Turks. Why should they speak Turkish?

'Yes,' Michael agreed gravely. 'Exactly like that. For us, some things are forever. Once our word is pledged, there is no turning back.'

Kelsey was left with plenty to think about as the seaplane winged south along the rocky west coast of Attica. Almost too aware of the man buckled into the seat at her left, she stared down, imprinting Greece on her memory. At Cape Sounion, a great temple dedicated to Poseidon poised majestically on a lonely point of land. Then, with the mainland behind them there was only the Aegean, dotted with the islands called the Cyclades. Rugged. Parched. Often desolate looking from above.

Michael named the islands as they passed over them: Kea. Kithnos. Siros. Places where only a people who took tradition and discipline and self-reliance to incredible lengths could have survived.

Each time he spoke, Kelsey turned her head to contemplate his calm, classic profile. He was, she knew, everything that Tucker Grant had not been. This man was totally dedicated to the people and principles he believed in. The woman who fell in love with him would be expected to honor a great many commitments.

In her heart lay the utter conviction that he would honor them too. That Michael Devos would never do anything halfway.

It was almost a relief to hear Zoe's perplexed voice from the rear seat. 'My mom's maps had the shapes of these islands on them, Uncle Michael. Why would she have said she was drawing them with her mind's eye?'

96

A baffled frown creased itself between Michael's black brows. 'Doesn't make sense to me, honey. Are you positive that's what she said?'

'Uh-huh. I remember for sure.'

Kelsey believed her. Zoe was one of the brightest youngsters she had ever encountered, with a memory that verged on photographic. On the other hand, professors were usually practical people who dealt in facts and expected their students to do so too. There were always a few visionaries on every campus, of course—thinkers whose special brilliance in their own field lifted them above the ordinary. They were the idealists who saw what might have been, or ought to be, as well as what actually was.

If Ione was this rare type of intellectual, Kelsey pondered, what would she have beheld with her mind's eye? What might she have drawn that wasn't visible to a pragmatic observer? More important still, how would that insight dovetail with the mystery she and Rupert and their small daughter had come to Greece to unravel?

Finding the answers to those questions would have to be postponed until later. Under Michael's deft touch, the seaplane began losing altitude. Moments later the skis touched down, causing hardly a ripple in the sparkling surface of the water. Before they had completely lost momentum, a sleek cruiser, captained by a man in his very early twenties, coasted forward. A minimum of jockeying brought boat and plane together.

As soon as the three of them had dropped down beside him, Stefanos tossed the jaunty red cap he'd been wearing to Michael. With a laugh he pointed to the bucket of fish he had caught while awaiting their arrival.

'They'll give you the look—and smell—of authenticity!' Then he grew quickly serious as he caught sight of the bandage slanting across Michael's temple. 'Trouble? I *knew* you should have let Dion and me come along when you went off to check out that much-too-tempting lead!'

'Either that or gone about the reconnaissance with far more caution. Next time I will, you may be certain.' Michael cocked his injured head toward the seaplane. 'I doubt anyone could have charted our course, but you might want to use a different heading for the return trip, just to make sure.'

'I can do better than that. As of this moment I'm on my way to Rhodes. Three ladies from Copenhagen have scheduled a week-long air/sea tour of the Sporades with me as their guide. I'm to pick them up off Lindos.' Stefanos slung a canvas duffel bag over his shoulder before flicking a last look around the trim fishing craft. 'Leave word at Andreas's shop if you finish with the boat before I get back. One of the family will take it off your hands. By the way, the charts you requested are all aboard. A few extra supplies, too, that I thought might come in handy.'

Something about the offhanded way he tossed out that piece of information made Kelsey suspect that the supplies he mentioned weren't the sort of provisions one purchased at the local grocery store. Out of courtesy to her the men had been speaking in English, but as they drifted back to the boat's stern, they lapsed into Greek for a final, low-voiced exchange. Then Stefanos swung himself up into the cockpit of the plane. Michael turned, striding purposefully back toward the boat's wheelhouse.

'Does everyone you know fly a plane?' Kelsey asked as the amphibian's powerful engine purred to life.

'No, of course not.' Michael looked briefly amused at the idea. 'I taught Dion and Stefanos to pilot a light plane three years ago. I'd just been discharged from the Navy and was paying a long-awaited visit to my parents' homeland before starting up my business in Seattle. Like me, neither of them was anxious to spend his life as a sponge fisherman, the way our fathers and grandfathers had done. They wanted to try something different in the way of guided tours. The venture has turned out to be very successful.'

'Fun too, I'll bet.' Kelsey couldn't quite hide a smile as she thought of the three ladies from

Denmark Stefanos had mentioned.

Zoe was drooping with fatigue. No wonder, Kelsey thought sympathetically. They had been on the go since early that morning. She pushed her suitcase up alongside the curving prow and stacked the cushy knapsack atop it to make a perch for the little girl. Then, as Michael charted a course for the distant shore, she leaned against the rail with her arm around Zoe, glad to have nothing to do for the moment except simply relax and enjoy their surroundings.

The Aegean was a rich, sapphire blue; the sky, where the hot sun hovered bright and blazing, only a half shade lighter. No wonder Icarus had fallen into the sea when he'd flown too high and the wax holding together his homemade wings melted, she mused, then shook her head. Here in Greece it was easy to forget what was legend, what mere fact.

For the first time it occurred to Kelsey that she didn't even know *where* in Greece they were. Being able to go with the flow to such an extent was not her usual style. Her matter-of-fact acceptance of one rushed segment after another of this odyssey was undoubtedly due to Michael Devos and to the confidence he inspired in her. With any other companion she would have been asking questions before even climbing into the car at Daphni.

The spot of land they'd been heading toward grew steadily more visible. From their original vantage point it had looked barren and sparsely inhabited. Suddenly Kelsey realized that for safety's sake they must have been approaching the island from its back side, for now, as they rounded a point, she knew where they were without having to ask.

Higher up against a brown-gold background brightened here and there by patches of brilliant red flowers was scattered a sparse assortment of houses. Farther down, rimming the harbor, buildings clustered thickly together; boon companions. Only in size did they seem to differ. Each structure was squarish, flat-roofed, so blindingly white that it hurt her eyes to stare directly at its rough, adobe-textured exterior. Even the slabstone streets filled with cement were white. Curtains, railings, pots of geraniums provided color in restrained doses, but the overall effect was dazzling.

Other islands might share those characteristics she'd so often pored over in travel posters, Kelsey knew, but one glimpse of the line of windmills with their distinctive, circular shapes and conical peaks covered in thatch, and their dozen sails swooping round and round in the breeze like never-pausing Ferris wheels settled the question without dispute.

Mykonos!

Even as the excited realization pounced, their boat angled in toward shore. All along the ridge the mills poised like sentries. Rather than proceeding around to the harbor, Michael seemed to be heading straight toward one of those unmistakable landmarks. He cut the motor; as they drifted noiselessly into the shallows, Kelsey saw that in the past others had made use of this landing spot. A sheltering niche was hollowed out where the boat could nose safely in among the rocks. An iron stanchion stood handy, ready to loop a painter around.

She boosted Zoe over the side when they had swayed to a halt, then took her hand for the steep ascent. Hefting the baggage, which now included the bucket of fish, Michael led the way.

Rough steps had been notched into the cliff. Up they climbed; up and up and up. Still the ponderous mill loomed above—forty, fifty, sixty feet over their heads. Kelsey decided she knew what caused people to see mirages. She kept her thoughts fixed on what must lie beyond the windmill. A house. Perhaps a hotel. *Some* oasis, she prayed, offering cool drinks of water and shelter from the blazing sun.

But Michael marched straight toward the windmill's thick, arched door. He pushed it open, then stood aside, waiting for them to enter.

'We're here,' he announced.

CHAPTER SIX

An hour later Philomena, the stout, cheery woman in charge of cooking and cleaning for the occupants of the windmill guest house, set a bowl of fresh figs on the table, then carried away the tray of dirty dishes. Her granddaughter, Cassandra, led a drowsy Zoe upstairs, promising to tuck her in for a nice long siesta in one of the reconverted mill's bedrooms. Replete from two helpings of moussaka, a tasty Greek casserole blending pasta, tomatoes, eggplant, and melted cheese, Kelsey finally found a chance to talk privately with Michael.

As she gazed around the large circular room, she still was hard pressed to believe her eyes. Cool, citrusy colors had been used to decorate the unusual space. Thick, terracotta walls kept the blistering heat at bay. She laughed now, remembering how appalled she had been earlier at the prospect of entering some dank, stuffy place crammed with machinery.

'Heavens,' she said admiringly, 'I always thought the windmills were used for grinding grain into flour.'

'That was their original purpose, of course. Many of them still do exactly that.' Michael helped himself to one of the dark, delicious figs. 'This place belongs to a great-aunt of Stefanos.

103

husband was a miller, but they had no sons to follow in his footsteps. When he died a few years ago, she decided to remodel the interior and rent it out to tourists during the season.'

He added that while only about eight thousand people lived on the island of Mykonos year-round, summer visitors increased the population to five times that number. Every square inch of housing was at a premium during July and August.

Kelsey hoped their unexpected arrival wasn't depriving someone else of the fun of staying here. Such picturesque accommodations would certainly highlight anyone's vacation.

She muffled a regretful sigh. Too bad they weren't on vacation themselves. But a far graver purpose had instigated their trip to Greece. At least the man across the table from her looked less exhausted, now that he'd had a chance to eat and rest. It was time she pried some answers from him.

'The day of our arrival in Athens you phoned to say you were just leaving to track down a promising lead you hoped might help you find Zoe's parents,' she began. 'Something went wrong, didn't it? I overheard what Stefanos said on the boat. It sounded as if that excursion proved to be more than just another dead end.'

'Oh, it was a dead end, all right. Almost literally, in fact.' Michael sounded grim as he touched the bandage on his forehead. 'Although when I set out, it seemed as if for once luck was sure to be on my side. You see, I found the trunk.'

'Paul Dürer's steamer trunk? Or should I say Paul Duval's?' Kelsey reminded herself that Rupert's great-grandfather had changed his name before leaving France. '*That* trunk?'

'The very same. I've since figured out that my sister located it first. Not long afterward someone else ran across it. Our nemesis, or someone working for him. They had it carted over to Athens, where I'd been snooping around, and arranged for me to stumble across it.'

Kelsey repressed a shiver. So he *had* been lured into a trap!

That trunk had made it possible for Ione and Rupert to retrace the route Paul Duval had followed with his mule cart forty years earlier. It had been noticeable enough that people tended to remember it even after all that time. 'The trail led from one isolated monastery to another,' Michael confided. 'At first they thought that since he was poor, he was just taking advantage of the free lodgings those religious communities offered to indigent travelers.'

'That wasn't really the case?'

'No, his purpose was much more straightforward. He wanted to talk to the monks.'

Michael said that these men had cut themselves off from the world to spend their lives in prayer and contemplation. 'But they were also there to study. Many of them are fine classical scholars. Rupert's ancestor went from place to place consulting with these learned men, asking them questions.'

'What about?'

'From the information Rupert and Ione were able to gather, he seemed to have hoped they could help him locate a particularly significant shrine.'

'Significant in what way?' Kelsey frowned. 'Temples like the Parthenon were all dedicated to the old deities. The Acropolis was even called the Sacred Rock. And that Sanctuary of Apollo existed at Daphni thousands of years ago.'

'You're right. From Mount Olympus on down, Greece is full of places where people once worshiped. But Paul Duval didn't ask any questions about Athena or Zeus or Apollo. He was only interested in finding some really special place that had been sacred to Aphrodite.'

Kelsey had grown up listening to the tales of Norse mythology. Now she was glad the stories about Odin, Thor, and Loki had stimulated an interest in the legends of other cultures too.

'The Romans called her Venus, didn't they? I wonder why Paul Duval picked her as his particular interest.'

'I could take a good guess.' The lively gleam in Michael's dark eyes announced that he'd given the matter plenty of thought. 'Duval knew he hadn't long to live. There was something he desperately wanted to do before he died. If his only reason for coming to Greece had been to visit the ancient sites he'd read about for so many years—and *if* there was nothing in that mysterious trunk except his personal belongings—then his concentration on one goddess over the others might have been a random choice. But if he was carrying something much more important—'

'Part of the treasure Heinrich Schliemann dug up at Troy?'

'Uh-huh. If that's what he had, then it's not surprising he was interested in Aphrodite. After all, she was the one who caused the Trojan War in the first place.'

Two great classical authors, Homer of Greece and Virgil of Rome, had written epic poems about that long conflict, Michael added. How much of the story was legend and how much actual history was anybody's guess. Troy *had* been a real place, a mighty city ruled by King Priam. Myth mingled with fact in the fanciful story of the beauty contest that Zeus appointed the king's son, Paris, to judge. One of the contestants didn't play fair. The goddess of love, Aphrodite, promised that if Paris presented her with the Golden Apple and proclaimed her the winner, she would see that the most beautiful mortal woman became his wife.

Soon after Aphrodite was awarded the coveted prize, Paris visited Sparta. There he fell madly in love with Helen. The royal beauty's face was said to have launched a thousand ships, because when he stole her away, her husband, King Menelaus, sent messengers to allies all over Greece, beseeching them to help him win her back. The resulting war lasted for ten years. Finally a clever ruse gave the Greeks the victory. Soldiers were smuggled into Troy, hidden in the massive wooden horse. They opened the gates for their comrades, who poured into the city and burned it to the ground.

Almost three thousand years later, Michael said, Schliemann used Homer's *Iliad* to locate Troy. The long-abandoned city was exactly where the ancient poet had said it would be, at the mouth of the Dardanelles in Asia Minor— now a part of modern-day Turkey.

Kelsey remembered how the indignant guide at the Acropolis had blamed the Turks for allowing Lord Elgin to remove so many beautiful art objects from Greece. 'Suppose that at the end of the war Paul Duval decided that a German museum had no right to possess Priam's treasure,' she thought aloud. 'Say he decided that justice could be served only by returning it to the part of the world where it had originated. But in retaliation for that business about the Elgin Marbles, he wanted Greece, not Turkey, to be the recipient of those precious things. It would be ironic, don't you think, if he decided to stash it in a spot that was once sacred to Aphrodite?'

With a laugh Michael declared that she would get along fine with his sister. 'That's exactly what Ione concluded he came here to do. What kept her awake nights was trying to figure out which of Aphrodite's shrines was to be honored with this gift. Apparently there were quite a few.'

Sadly most of the scholars Paul Duval had consulted were no longer living when Ione started her search forty years later. Michael said that after months of research she had a pretty good notion of what the answer might be.

'What she did was make an educated guess. There wasn't any proof, so she didn't share that information with anyone except Rupert. They headed for Athens. She wanted to consult some very old manuscripts in one of the historical museums there.' He glanced toward the upper story of the windmill, where his niece lay sleeping. 'Ione drew those charts Zoe remembers seeing while they were en route to the capital.'

'She told me the islands on her mother's maps looked "crowdeder together" than the way they appeared in my atlas,' Kelsey confided. 'How do you suppose that fits in with Ione's comment that she was drawing things "with her mind's eye"?'

'It certainly didn't mean that she was just doodling. Ione insisted on complete accuracy when she made notes or drew charts.' After a moment's thoughtful silence Michael started to add something else. Then he shook his head. 'I do have a glimmer of an idea,' he admitted, 'but airplanes are my specialty, not the world as it might have looked a long time ago. I'd rather check some facts with an expert before going out on a limb and starting to make wild guesses.'

Guesswork or not, Kelsey wished he were willing to share his ideas with her. She wouldn't have minded helping to brainstorm the problem to see if they could come up with some feasible solutions. But she couldn't claim to be an expert in Ione's field, either, so she had no basis for asking.

'Then tell me about the trunk.' She returned the conversation to its starting point. 'Where did you run across it?'

'At a shoddy antique shop in Piraeus. That's the seaport a few miles west of Athens, where all the ferryboat lines originate.' He could hardly have missed it, since the massive piece of luggage was displayed in the shop's front window. Sheepishly Michael confessed that he had been so elated to spot a tattered sticker glued on its top, proving that the trunk had once traveled on the same long-defunct freighter that brought Paul Duval to Greece, he hadn't even suspected a trick.

'The character in charge of the place told me he'd located the trunk down in Ios. It wasn't valuable, he said. He'd picked it up only to use for transporting a group of icons he'd bought on the same trip. At the time I thought he'd done me an enormous favor by telling me the island it came from.' Disgusted with himself for being so gullible, Michael grimaced. 'Later I wondered why he hadn't even twisted my arm to buy something while I was in his shop. But by then bullets were flying around my head. It was too late to ask questions.'

The word 'bullets' struck dread into Kelsey's heart. One man had already been killed by a hit-and-run driver. Attempts had been made to kidnap Zoe. Now Michael had come within a fraction of an inch—

She bit her lip. 'I've never heard of Ios. Did somebody follow you there?'

'Worse. He arrived ahead of time, to lie in wait.'

Michael was certain that the sniper had not been working alone. As he ran to catch the ferry after phoning Kelsey at the Acantha, a man almost made him miss the boat.

'I was charging toward the ramp when a stranger hailed me and started asking questions. While I didn't like to be impolite, he was blocking my path; I finally had to tell him to get out of the way.' They had both wound up jumping aboard the ferry just as it was pulling away from the dock.

Michael shrugged. 'At the time it seemed like one of those minor aggravations that you soon forget. But what happened a few hours later was a different story.'

Ios, he explained, was one of the most remote of the Cyclades, the islands strewn for a couple of hundred miles between the Greek mainland and Crete's massive bulk to the south. Ferry service down that way was infrequent and slow.

'You've heard of the "milk run" made by trains that halt at every whistle-stop? That's a good description of the ferry to Ios. Most of the other passengers disembarked at Naxos. After that, the boat meandered from one tiny speck of land to another.' Michael touched his head. 'Believe me, I won't forget that last one.'

Livestock was carried on a lower deck of the ferry. It was late in the day, but still very hot, when they put in at some nameless rock. There, a shepherd was waiting to drive a balky herd of goats aboard.

'It was easy to see we were in for a tedious delay. No one was keen on standing around downwind of those stubborn critters. Everybody remaining aboard climbed out onto the pier to get away from all the commotion.'

Most of his fellow passengers walked over

and bought something to eat at the small food stand near the water. Michael himself hadn't been hungry. Just bored, he said, and in need of some exercise.

'I started jogging slowly along the waterfront. I couldn't have gone more than twenty or thirty yards when I heard footsteps thundering up behind me. Next thing I knew, someone shoved me off the path. As I was falling, I heard shots whistle past my ear.'

Michael added that he had struck his head on a rock when he fell, then must have lost consciousness for a few minutes. 'But just as I was going down, I caught a quick glimpse of the guy who'd tried to keep me from boarding the ferry at the start of the line.'

'He's the one who pushed you?'

'Yep. He didn't stick around to take a bow, though—*or* to explain how he happened to guess that there'd be someone up on the hillside with a sniperscope on his rifle, just waiting for me to come along.'

When he came to, Michael said, he was ringed by a crowd of onlookers. His rescuer had vanished. No one got a close-up look at the would-be assassin.

Anger flared in Kelsey's blue eyes. 'What about the shepherd?'

'Don't miss much, do you?' Michael observed, pleased at her quick uptake. 'After the captain put his first-aid kit away, I had a little talk with the owner of the goats. He
113

seemed as bewildered as everybody else. All he could tell me was that, the previous day, a buyer had offered him a generous sum for the whole herd. He collected his pay up front. All he had to do was drive them down to the dock and get them on the ferry the next day.'

But on arrival in Ios, he added in a telling tone, no one had shown up to claim the goats.

'So the whole thing was a put-up job. Whoever arranged the diversion must have felt certain everyone would get off the ferry while the animals were being loaded.' Kelsey shook her head. 'Michael, that other passenger had to have known ahead of time what was going to happen. First he did his best to keep you from catching the boat. When that didn't work, he rode along, followed you up the path, and saved your life with a shove.'

'Weird, isn't it? The kid running the snack bar saw him and another man pile into a powerful motorboat and take off at full speed immediately after the incident.'

'First someone wants you killed; then they don't. What do you suppose it means?'

'That I've used up one of my nine lives,' Michael grumbled. 'Something else, though— that tiny island didn't run to anything as modern as phone service.'

To Kelsey, that fact explained a lot. 'So once a trap was arranged, there would have been no quick way to call it off. The only way to keep that marksman from using you for target practice was for another of the conspirators to go along on the ferry ride and try to warn his cohort off.' She scowled. 'He didn't quite succeed, though at least he kept you from getting shot. Was he a Greek?'

'No.' Michael sounded surprised, as though this were a point he hadn't had a chance to consider yet. 'He wasn't an American, either, although he spoke in English when he approached me at the dock in Piraeus. He might have been British—Welsh, maybe. It was an odd accent, hard to put your finger on.'

'I wonder how he knew *you* weren't a local.' But the answer to that was too easy. Michael had been watched. Steered into that antique shop, then followed to the dock when he took the bait. The non-Greek had known exactly whose life he was saving. A sudden thought hit her. 'How odd! That's twice an antique shop has entered the picture.'

'So it is,' Michael agreed thoughtfully. 'The Etruscan jewelry Alec Westerlin was hired to trace had turned up in a shop in Marseilles. That's how he came to check back to the Berlin Museum and find out what else never surfaced after the war. Incidentally, the shop where I spotted the trunk is temporarily out of business. When I went back last night, there was a padlock on the door and a sign in the window saying the place was closed for vacation.'

'How   convenient.   The   people

masterminding this plot must have guessed you'd be back looking for answers.'

'Or blood. They seem able to handle things with a snap of their fingers.' From the beginning, Michael added, it had been obvious that someone both rich and powerful was involved. Kidnappers had been dispatched to Florida with seemingly as little problem as an assassin had been sent to eliminate a man on an Athens street. 'The one silver lining to all this is that by being decoyed off to Ios, I wasn't able to come collect you at the airport.'

Kelsey understood his meaning. Zoe's masquerade as Jason would have done little good, had they been seen in her uncle's company.

'Speaking of Ios,' she said, 'were you able to trace the trunk once you and the goats arrived there?'

He nodded. 'Believe it or not, the guy in the antique shop had told the truth about where it came from. I imagine he knew I wasn't slated to live long enough to investigate. And, by the way, if I never hear another word about goats, it will be too soon.'

Michael had stayed overnight in Ios before taking the ferry back the next day. After checking into a nondescript hotel, he headed for the waterfront *taverna* that had been described to him. The middle-aged woman in charge of the place declared that the trunk had belonged to her family since she was a small child.

'In those days her widowed mother ran the place,' Michael said. 'During the lean years following the war she took in lodgers to help pay expenses. Even though he had no money, she was kindhearted enough to find a bed for a sick old man who had showed up out of nowhere. He insisted that he didn't want charity, that he had a trunk to trade for a few weeks' board and room.'

He added that there'd been no need for Paul Duval to make further arrangements. Soon after he came to Ios, the illness that had first been diagnosed in Germany took its toll. He was buried in the small local cemetery.

Kelsey wondered whether Rupert's elderly ancestor had managed to achieve his final goal. 'Was there anything in the trunk when he gave it to his landlady?'

'Only a few odds and ends of clothing.'

Over time, the trunk had served a number of purposes in the household. Eventually it became part of the *taverna*'s decor. Nowadays the waterfront café/bar catered to the yachting crowd and was done up in a nautical theme.

No doubt it had been draped with fishnets and sprinkled with sand, Kelsey presumed. 'You mentioned something about your sister finding the trunk first?'

Michael nodded. 'When I took a snapshot of her and Rupert out of my wallet, the woman recognized them at once. They came to talk to

117

her about three weeks ago. While they were there, they asked about Paul Duval. They'd seen the notation of his death in the church records. When she showed them the trunk with its faded old sticker, they looked as though they'd just found the last piece in a jigsaw puzzle.'

That same day his sister and brother-in-law had left Ios, Michael added. 'Then last week someone showed up saying he dealt in antiques. He offered her such a good price for the trunk, she couldn't refuse.'

Once again, that lavish use of money. Kelsey felt a trifle sick when she reflected that the only reason the trunk had been purchased and removed from that *taverna* was so that Michael could be lured into a trap. Then, capriciously it seemed, his rich and powerful adversary had decided that he wasn't to die, after all.

How confusing this all was! She grasped at another straw. 'What about Aphrodite? Did a shrine in her honor ever exist on Ios?'

'I checked with several knowledgeable people there on the island. No one I spoke with had ever heard of such a place.' As if attempting to keep a headache at bay, Michael massaged the back of his neck. 'Though I hate to admit it, I'm just about out of ideas.'

He looked so exhausted that Kelsey yearned to draw his dark head down on her shoulder and assure him that everything was bound to turn out fine. But that might be far from the truth. Besides, she had no call to do any such thing. They were here together out of a mutual concern for the little girl upstairs, nothing more.

Actually, even Pollyanna would have found it hard to say anything optimistic at the moment. After popping up briefly on Ios, Rupert and Ione had disappeared again. And their adversaries seemed to have them boxed in at every corner.

Michael must have sensed the gulp she forced down. From across the table he sent her an apologetic look. 'I'm sorry for dragging you into this mess, Kelsey. Back in Seattle I didn't realize things would get so out of hand.'

There was plenty to worry him without fretting about her. 'Well, I'm glad I came along,' she declared staunchly. 'The situation looks gloomy right now because we're both so tired. I'm betting that Zoe will be able to give you a whole new perspective on where her parents might have gone. No need beating your head against the wall until you've had a chance to talk with her.'

'About those islands that were "crowdeder together"?' A reluctant grin dragged at the corners of Michael's mouth. 'Let's hope it all makes more sense after a few hours' shut-eye.'

He headed off to the lower-level room the housekeepers had prepared for him. Climbing the spiral staircase to the top of the reconverted windmill, Kelsey conquered the urge to look

119

back. Some men would have felt the need to act macho no matter what, to pretend they had everything under control, whether they were facing a blank wall or not. Michael was honest enough to suggest that his best might not have been good enough.

But he wasn't beaten yet, she assured herself fiercely. Together they would see this thing through!

*   *   *

Dinner, served unusually early by Greek standards, featured baked fish as the entree. Kelsey enjoyed every morsel of the flaky seafood, but declined the honey-and-nut baklava as tactfully as she was able.

Zoe loved the rich dessert, though. She delighted Philomena by munching her way through two of the sticky-sweet confections.

Leaving his niece to enjoy the treat, Michael opted for coffee later on. Although he'd grown progressively more quiet as the meal went on, now he tendered an invitation. 'I need to go down and get those charts out of the boat before dark. Want to come with me, Kelsey?'

'Love to.' She had more than one reason for accepting. An energetic trudge down that cliff and back again would probably be the only way she was ever going to get her slacks zipped tomorrow. No one could accuse Greek food of being low in calories!

120

Shimmering across the placid sea as it dropped beyond the horizon, the flaming sun transformed earth, water, and sky into a wraparound rainbow of color. From a distance Kelsey caught the faint thrum of music. Mykonos, coming alive for the evening.

The necessity of watching her footing gave her time for no more than a single wistful thought about the lively scene sure to be taking place down by the harbor. Dust stirred, pebbles rolled as they clambered down the last few yards of the path.

Michael swung himself lithely aboard the boat, then turned, spanning her waist with two strong hands to boost her over the side. The keel swayed. Her feet lost their balance. Or was it her head? It seemed to be whirling like the giddy sails of one of those windmills high on the ridge. Being this close to Michael Devos was more than a little unsettling.

With another man Kelsey might have looked away, drawn a breath to get her bearings. But their identical heights proved her undoing. There was no place to gaze except directly into his eyes. Once held by those sparkling warm depths, she was lost.

Slowly Michael drew her closer and inclined his head. Hard sinews rippled beneath her fingertips as Kelsey slid her arms around his neck. Kissing him seemed more right, more natural, than anything she had ever done before.

After a long moment he drew back a fraction. His whisper grazed her lips. 'I've been wanting to do that since the first time we met.'

Careful, Kelsey warned herself. *Lose your heart to this one, and it's gone for good.* Kisses were one thing, commitment another. All his energies were pledged to following through on the search that had brought him to Greece. She wasn't willing to settle for a fling, a brief summer romance.

'Must have been those cookies.' With a deliberate effort she kept her tone light. 'Grandma Helga always claimed their aroma was more potent than perfume.'

'I knew it had to be culture shock.' Michael's comment sounded whimsical. 'After twenty-eight years of baklava, I got done in by a batch of Norwegian spice cookies.'

In the shadows his smile faded. Resolutely he wedged a little more distance between their two bodies. 'Kelsey, there's nothing I'd like better than to spend the next few weeks comparing all the other things we never had in common. I'm sorry that won't be possible. You have to go home. Tomorrow.'

CHAPTER SEVEN

By the time Kelsey awoke next morning, it was almost nine. Small wonder, she thought,

122

peering groggily at the clock. It must have been nearly dawn when she finally fell asleep. For hours after rushing upstairs she had tossed and turned, trying without success to think of some way to persuade Michael to change his mind.

Following the ambush in which he had narrowly escaped with his life, he had made the decision to send her home. There was no point in both of them being trapped in the line of fire. When asked, he admitted that Zoe would not be returning to the States with Kelsey. If ever he was to learn what had happened to her parents, he needed his niece's help. Besides, the kidnap attempts in Florida had proved that she was no safer in America than she would be in Greece.

But Kelsey was different. An outsider. There was no reason, Michael insisted, for her to run the risk of becoming further involved with the problems his family had blundered into.

She had objected—vehemently. He refused to budge.

'We've been lucky so far. Don't you understand, Kelsey? Someone rich and powerful and ruthless is determined to get his hands on whatever it was Paul Duval brought to Greece in that trunk. But at least he hasn't singled you out as another of his targets. Yet. You're getting out of here before that happens. I refuse to go on risking your life.'

'Darn it, I'm responsible for my own life!'

'Not this time.' He gave his head an adamant

123

shake. 'If I had really considered the consequences, I would never have dragged you into this. But I'd be lying if I said I was sorry we ever met. Someday, after we're home and this nightmare is just a terrifying memory...'

'Never mind, Michael.' Kelsey managed to force the denial out through a throat that ached from the effort to keep from crying. 'There's no point discussing the future when you've made it clear I'm not welcome to be part of your present.'

He made a hurt sound of protest. Kelsey ignored the muted groan as obstinately as she avoided his outstretched hand. Catapulting over the side of the boat, she began to scramble up the path without a backward look. Twice she stumbled, bruising her knee and scraping her arm on the unyielding rock. The minor injuries weren't nearly so painful as Michael's rejection. With gritty determination she forged upward to level ground.

At the top Kelsey spent several distraught moments fighting for composure before going inside to tell Zoe good night.

'I've decided to take a bath and turn in early.' She gave the little girl a quick, affectionate hug. 'You had such a good, long nap today, you should still be wide-awake—all set to help your uncle with those maps the two of you are going to look at together. Think hard, okay, honey? Some tiny detail you remember might turn out to be a very important clue.'

'Sure, I know. I've been trying. More than anything I want to find my mom and dad.'

The earnest assurance ripped at Kelsey's heartstrings. More than anything, she wanted to stay and help too. But she wasn't to be allowed that privilege. Barely managing to keep her voice steady, she promised to see Zoe the next morning at breakfast.

Now, hurrying down the stairs, she realized with sick certainty that she'd broken her word. Breakfast was long over. Except for Philomena and herself, the windmill guest house was empty of occupants.

In a mixture of Greek, gestures, and bits of broken English, the housekeeper conveyed the information that her granddaughter had gone off with the others to show them the way to the doctor's house.

'Doctor!' Kelsey's quick moan betrayed her agitation. 'Was one of them sick? Hurt? That gash on Michael's head didn't start bleeding again, did it?'

Luckily Cassandra returned just then. The pretty sixteen-year-old was studying English in school. She managed to make sense out of the distressed queries. No, *thespinas*, the child was not ill. No, the *kyrie*'s head was fine. He no longer even wore the bandage. It was not a medical doctor they had gone to see, but a—

At a loss for this translation, Cassandra snatched up a book from the end table. She

125

buried her nose in it, evidently attempting to look studious.

It had been a long time since Kelsey had last played charades, but this bit of miming seemed easily interpreted. 'Oh, you mean the kind of doctor who teaches! A professor?'

Cassandra appeared to nod and shake her head negatively at the same time. Not exactly a professor, though Dr Youvis was a most learned man. The *kyrie* had called him— Struggling to communicate, she came up with a word that sounded like 'archaeologist.'

Comprehension flooded over Kelsey. Of course! Archaeologists studied things that were old—civilizations that had flourished thousands of years ago. Michael must be hoping that Dr Youvis would be able to tell him something about one of Aphrodite's shrines. Either that or Zoe had succeeded in giving him some new perspective. If anyone could guess what Ione had seen with her mind's eye, it was likely to be a fellow classicist.

The *kyrie*, Cassandra went on, had said to tell *thespinas* Anderson to have a pleasant morning. He and the little one would see her at noon.

To share a farewell lunch, then speed her on her way, Kelsey guessed. The notion weighed like an anvil on her sagging spirits. Michael couldn't wait to get rid of her. He had probably already arranged passage for her on a ferry returning to Athens this afternoon. From there

126

she would be expected to head for the airport without delay.

Last evening she had used her most convincing arguments without the slightest effect on the stubborn stand he had taken. Kelsey admitted that the chances of coming up with a valid excuse for staying on in Greece between now and the time she saw him again hovered between pitiful and zilch.

If she had paid her own way, things would have been different. She could have dug in her heels and done as she pleased. But escorting Zoe to Athens had been a business arrangement made through her cousin's firm. Refusing point-blank to obey his instructions would probably constitute breach of contract or something equally lawsuit-inviting, and she wasn't about to bring that down on Joanna's head. She was just as devoted to her family as Michael was to his.

Which was why, Kelsey decided with a perverse tilt to her chin, she was not about to return home without some sort of souvenirs for her favorite relatives. Michael wouldn't be back for almost another three hours. That didn't leave much time to get acquainted with this delightful little island, but certainly she could find a better way to spend her morning than moping around in a windmill!

Within ten minutes she had changed into a pair of red linen slacks, cut to flare stylishly out at midcalf. The coordinating white blouse, trimmed in the same vivid hue, had, like the slacks, been a gift from her parents upon their return from a Norwegian vacation at Eastertime. Her leather sandals were the sort of footgear a European on holiday might choose to wear, and her long blond hair had been brushed out to bounce loosely across her shoulders.

Not so long ago Michael had suggested that she and Zoe mingle with the many Scandinavian tourists who enjoyed summering in Greece. Now, though there was no need here to adopt a disguise, she found the idea appealing. *Frøken* Kelsey Anderson, whose ancestors, at least, had come from Oslo, was on her way to take a close-up look at Mykonos!

By the time she had walked the scant mile downhill, fourteen separate motor scooters had skidded to a halt beside her. To each of the attractive young men who beseeched her to accept a ride to wherever it was she might be headed, Kelsey replied, '*Ohi, efharisto*'—No, thank you—but with such a pleasant smile that several of her would-be knights-errant didn't give up for blocks. It was a morale-building introduction to the town, which proved to be every bit as charming and good-looking as its male population.

Even the front steps of the closely clustered homes had been whitewashed. Against the dazzling monochrome background, doors, windows, and balcony rails painted red and blue formed a cheery kaleidoscope of contrast to the overall white. Narrow alleys wove around the homes in baffling, serpentine fashion. Kelsey remembered reading that these had originally been designed to foil marauding pirates. With a grin she observed that today the only freebooters in sight were the many cats, all alert for a handout.

While it was far too early for any of the island's famous visitors to be out and about, the doors of countless boutiques, art galleries, and pastry shops stood invitingly ajar. Kelsey meandered from one side of the fascinating street to the other as she continued downhill, absorbing the sights and sounds and aromas that always in the future would remind her of Mykonos. Her ears picked up a rhythmic 'click, click, click.' Ahead of her, three men intent on a business discussion were running small chains of amber beads through their fingers.

Worry beads, Michael had called them. Links of the smooth stones were used by men all over the Middle East to soothe away tensions.

The recollection of Michael Devos prompted Kelsey to walk a little faster. There was so much to see and so little time! High on her list of priorities was the harbor. And Petros, of course, the cantankerous pelican who waddled about the waterfront all day, cadging fish and allowing his photo to be snapped.

The water drew her forward. Rocking on the flood tide, a fleet of freshly painted small boats nudged the wharf. Kelsey leaned against the thigh-high stone seawall, gazing past the small fishing craft at an impressive yacht riding at anchor further out. Before she had a chance to more than wonder which of the fabulously wealthy Greek shipping magnates it might belong to, a magnificent cruise ship, as dazzlingly white as Mykonos itself, steamed into view. Nine or ten decks high, bright pennants fluttering from needle-pointed prow to soaring stack and back to rounded stern, she made a stately entrance into the mouth of the bay.

Kelsey shielded her eyes. The name *Golden Odyssey* was lettered in that same rich hue on either side of the sharp bow.

It soon became apparent that the huge, elegant vessel intended to come no closer. Kelsey's disappointment was echoed by the British schoolboy who, with his father, had paused to watch from a few feet farther on down the seawall. 'Why doesn't she hurry and dock?' the impatient child demanded.

'The harbor's too shallow. A ship that size would risk snagging her propellers on the bottom if she ventured any farther in.' The boy's father pointed to a good-sized, flat-bottomed launch now approaching the luxury liner. 'The passengers won't miss out on a chance to come ashore, though. That smaller boat will be shuttling them back and forth all day long.'

Hearing this, it dawned on Kelsey that Mykonos would soon be jam-packed with cruise passengers. There looked to be hundreds of people already lining the decks of the *Golden Odyssey*, awaiting their turn at a seat in the launch. Prudently she decided that if she was to have a chance at gift shopping, it would be smart to get started before every store on the island was inundated by crowds.

The problems she had encountered stuffing everything back into her suitcase in Athens had caused her to give some thought to the problem of space. It would be best, Kelsey concluded, if everything she bought here on Mykonos was small enough to fit into a single box she could carry aboard the plane. On the way down to the harbor, a specialty boutique with a large assortment of decorative tiles displayed in the window had caught her eye. Hand-painted with colorful scenes from ancient and modern-day Greece, they'd then been glazed to a high sheen.

By the time the first launchload of cruise passengers came hurrying up Mattheou-Andronikou Street, Kelsey's selection was complete. The dozen eight-inch-square tiles she had chosen could either make unique wall hangings or serve as trivets for placing hot dishes on the table. The several sets of small round tiles she'd picked out would be ideal for use as coasters. Her family would love them, she thought, endorsing three of her travelers' checks to pay for the purchase.

They did all fit into one box too, though it was heavier than she'd anticipated. Pausing outside the door of the shop, Kelsey took a firmer grip on her string-bound burden and wondered whether there was any such thing as bus service on the island. The prospect of lugging twenty pounds of ceramic tile back up the hill to the windmill was rather daunting.

An astonished exclamation jolted her out of her reverie before she could decide what to do about getting back. 'Well, for heaven's sake! This *is* a surprise!' cried a familiar voice.

'Sarah!' Kelsey looked up to find her congenial seatmate from the London-to-Athens flight staring at her in amazement. With a chuckle she surveyed the load of packages in the other woman's arms. 'How nice to see you again! What are you trying to do—buy out every store on Mykonos?'

'I suppose it looks that way, but the things here are utterly irresistible.' The chic Englishwoman lifted an eyebrow at the sight of Kelsey's heavy parcel. 'Apparently I'm not the only one who thinks so. What say we go have a cup of coffee and set this stuff down while we catch our breath?'

The two of them headed back down the block toward the waterfront. Unfortunately,

132

however, they were too late to find one of the charming, umbrella-topped tables available. Passengers from the cruise ship had spilled ashore in droves and were thronging the sidewalk cafes as well as all the nearby shops.

'Oh, bother! Never mind; I've a much better idea, anyway,' Sarah declared. 'My gentleman friend works for the man who owns that spectacular yacht out there. One of *Naiad's* crew ran me ashore and promised to wait while I shopped. We'll have him take us away from this mob to enjoy our refreshments out on deck.' Starting off toward the pier at a fast clip, she turned on her heel as Kelsey hesitated. 'What's the matter? Mr Van Ryn has a superb chef. Pastries are one of his specialties.'

'Sarah, that's a lovely offer. If only there were time, I'd take you up on it in a shot. But I'm committed to a luncheon date I simply can't break.'

'Nonsense, it's barely eleven.' Sarah waved the protest aside with a beautifully manicured hand, then clutched at her slipping parcels. 'You'll be back in plenty of time. The boat ride takes less than five minutes.'

Kelsey had gone off without breakfast that morning; the mention of coffee and pastries was hard to refuse. She decided that with her shopping finished in one fell swoop, she could spare half an hour. Afterward she'd find a taxi to take her directly back to the windmill.

The motorboat into which they stepped was

a sleek, speedy craft. Kelsey balanced the box of tiles on her lap as she sank into one of the plush, cushioned seats. Sarah arranged herself comfortably and made a sharp comment about the noise level. The dark-shirted sailor from *Naiad* shrugged and snapped off the radio he'd been listening to, then shoved the throttle forward.

Once music stopped blaring in her ear, Kelsey enjoyed the swift ride. She'd been brought up around boats. Every July since she was a teenager she'd helped to crew for the annual Seafair races on Lake Washington. With a twinge of regret she recalled that as usual she'd be home for the festival instead of here with Michael and Zoe.

A solid-looking gangplank had been lowered from *Naiad*'s lowest deck to a gently bobbing platform. After making the boat fast, the sailor vaulted out and helped the women alight. Moments later they were aboard the gorgeous yacht that Kelsey had first admired from the seawall.

In the lead, Sarah ascended a carpeted companionway, then angled through a magnificently furnished lounge complete with grand piano. Kelsey caught glimpses of fine woods and queen-sized sofas, silken hangings, and breathtaking oil paintings before following the other woman through a heavy door out onto the attractive open deck. There, tables and chairs had been arranged in inviting clusters, and massive water jars planted with colorful summer blooms gave the space the look of a lush private terrace.

A muscular, dark-haired man had been leaning against the polished teakwood rail. Turning, he gave a half-exasperated shake of his head when he saw the packages spilling out of Sarah's grasp. Then, at the sight of the tall young woman bringing up the rear, his face went curiously still.

'You'll never guess who I met in town,' Sarah bubbled excitedly. 'I told you about the American I sat next to on the plane, remember? Here she is in person, believe it or not. Kelsey, meet Geoff.'

Geoff seemed rooted to the spot for a few seconds. Then, stepping forward, he clasped Kelsey's outstretched hand while appraising her with the sort of conjectural regard the Wolf might have fastened upon Red Riding Hood.

'Yes, indeed,' he said in a musing tone. 'Sarah mentioned what good company you were. You and...' He shot a questing glance over her shoulder. 'Your child isn't with you today.'

'No,' Kelsey responded acerbically as she retrieved her hand. 'He isn't.'

If Sarah had considered the sleeping 'Jason' good company, she must have been hard up for companionship. After a flattering comment or two about the yacht, Kelsey caught the other woman's eye. 'You were certainly right. This is

135

a glorious place to enjoy our coffee.'

Sarah seemed almost to have forgotten the pressing invitation she'd extended on shore. Now, hearing the tactful reminder, she unloaded her parcels onto the nearest table and smiled at Geoff. 'We're both famished. Do call the steward, will you, darling? Ask him to bring us a tray of midmorning goodies at once.'

'What a nice idea! I'm sure Mr Van Ryn will wish to join you.' For a moment before turning away, he returned his unsettling gaze to Kelsey. 'He's a great admirer of beauty. He should find you ... fascinating.'

Having taken an instant dislike to Sarah's 'gentleman friend,' Kelsey felt a surge of relief when he strode off. She had no desire to be found 'fascinating,' by the yacht owner or anyone else. More disturbing than even that last suggestive comment was the way he'd raised the subject of her young traveling companion. She wondered exactly what Sarah had told him about her seatmates.

When eyeing the yacht from the seawall, she'd fantasized about it belonging to a Greek shipping magnate. That was obviously not the case. Kelsey didn't know who or what Mr Van Ryn was; all she really wanted was to get off his boat as soon as she could gracefully manage to depart. Only the speculation sure to result kept her from leaving this instant. For the sake of the people she'd grown so fond of, she couldn't risk causing gossip.

Might as well make the best of the situation, now that she was here. Setting her box of tiles down next to Sarah's packages, Kelsey shot a rueful glance at her hand. Contact with Geoff had made her skin crawl.

'I'm positively grubby,' she said. 'May I use the powder room, please?'

Sarah looked perplexed, then broke into a laugh. 'Oh, you mean the loo! Of course you may. Go right on back through the salon, then second left.'

'Second left,' Kelsey found, led down a short hallway before opening into a well-appointed rest room. The sink was marble, the mirror beveled and enclosed in a burnished gold frame to match the taps. Opaque glass covered a pair of tightly latched portholes. As she turned off the spigot and reached for a towel, it occurred to her that the room must be vented to the outside. She could distinctly hear Sarah's high heels clicking across the deck at the approach of a heavier step.

'Where the devil is she?' the man called Geoff demanded.

'Calm down; she'll be right back. She just went to visit the loo. Isn't this the most amazing luck?' Sarah crowed. 'I couldn't believe my eyes when I saw her standing there.'

'Yes,' he agreed in a nasty tone. 'For a change one of your shopping expeditions turned out to be worth the effort. The boss might even decide to forgive you for fouling up your last assignment.'

'I've explained that time and again!' Sarah hurled back an angry retort. 'My instructions were quite explicit. I was to sit next to an American woman traveling in the company of a seven-year-old girl and not let them out of my sight for an instant. Well, I've *told* you and Van Ryn too—there was no such pair on the plane! The brat this woman had in tow was a *boy*. And I doubt his age was anywhere near as old as seven!'

The vehemence in her voice knocked the breath out of Kelsey. They were talking about Zoe and her!

'Come off it, Sarah. That boy-girl switch was a clever bit of misdirection, and you fell for it. Threw a real spanner in the works, I tell you,' Geoff grumbled. 'The boss had me rig up an elaborate scam to lure Devos to an out-of-the-way place where he could be permanently dispatched. At the last minute, because of your dimwittedness, we had to call the whole thing off. Without the kid in our hands to lead us to wherever her parents are hiding, we didn't dare let anything happen to the uncle. When I couldn't keep him from catching the ferry, I had to hop aboard and go along. Later it was all I could do to elbow my way through a smelly herd of goats in time to keep Nico from filling him full of holes.'

Kelsey found herself clutching the marble sink with trembling fingers. Michael, she thought numbly, had known a lot about his adversaries. That they were rich and powerful and utterly ruthless. He just hadn't realized how close they were.

She sent up a prayer of thanksgiving for Zoe's inspired idea to cut her hair and play the part of a boy. 'Jason's' masquerade wouldn't have fooled anyone for very long. It hadn't needed to. By hoodwinking Sarah, the simple disguise had saved Michael's life.

Now it was her own turn to try and pull a bit of life-or-death chicanery. This self-serving group would have no interest in what happened to a teacher from Seattle, so long as she told them everything they wanted to know. And she knew far too much for Michael and Zoe's safety.

There wasn't a second to lose. It was amazing that Sarah hadn't already begun to wonder why she hadn't yet returned from the 'loo.' She had to get off this yacht—fast!

Closing the door very quietly behind her, Kelsey hurried down the short hallway, then turned left to retrace the route she and Sarah had taken when coming aboard. Twice, while making her way along the lower deck, she heard voices muffled behind closed doors. But the alarm still hadn't been given, and no one approached to challenge her.

The hatch to the gangplank stood open, as it had earlier. Earnestly wishing she'd worn something less eye-catching in color, Kelsey crept down the steps, onto the platform, and reached to fumble with the towline. The sailor had pulled the rope tight; it took her an anxious moment to get it untied from the mooring cleat. Then, still clutching the shoulder bag she'd carried with her all the way, she stepped down, into the motorboat.

Her first impulse was to head for shore with all the power she could coax from the speedy little boat. If she did so, though, the fat would be in the fire at once. From where they stood on the starboard deck, Sarah and her gentleman friend would spot her the instant she broke clear from *Naiad*'s shadow. They could hardly help it. At the moment, only one other vessel could be seen plying the wide expanse of water. The launch, which for the past hour had been shuttling cruise passengers back and forth, had just put out from the Mykonos wharf. The too-capable Geoff would simply lower another small boat and thunder along in her wake. She might make it as far as the pier, but even that would be chancy.

Michael and Zoe deserved a better effort from her than that. With a gulp Kelsey realized how very fond she had become of both of them. There had to be a way of muddying the waters. She had to keep this unscrupulous bunch guessing, at least for a while.

First things first. Right now she needed to slip out of sight without attracting attention.

To her eternal gratitude, the engine started

140

without a sputter. Letting the boat barely idle to keep noise to a minimum, she edged away from *Naiad*. Since it seemed impossible to go forward without disastrous consequences, she would simply have to go backward. Seaward. Pushing the throttle slightly forward, she headed toward the massive bulk of *Golden Odyssey*, riding majestically at anchor farther out in the channel.

Every minute seemed like an eternity. Kelsey kept her bright head bent low over the wheel, trying to stay as inconspicuous as possible. Sternly she resisted the impulse to look back. The die was cast now, for better or for worse. All she could do was cross her fingers that her box of tiles, sitting openly on the table next to the half dozen bags containing Sarah's purchases, was continuing to lull suspicion, giving the impression that she was still aboard the yacht.

A wide, sturdy platform had been connected to the ocean liner's lower deck. It formed a secure walkway for people transferring from ship to launch. Kelsey idled the motorboat up to the rear of the wooden float, then hopped out onto it. With a quick motion she reached back, and yanked the control lever down to full power. The now-empty motorboat roared away, arrowing toward open water at a fast clip. At that rate, she concluded in satisfaction, it would run out of fuel long before reaching the Turkish shore. She hoped that whoever

141

salvaged the abandoned craft out there on the high seas would be able to make good use of it.

The maneuver had taken only seconds. Luckily, the crew of the *Golden Odyssey* was tending strictly to business, while the paying customers were preoccupied with enjoying every moment of their vacation to the fullest. Passengers were stepping out onto the platform, intent on boarding the launch for the short excursion in to Mykonos. Amazingly, no one even seemed to notice the newcomer, or the unconventional method by which she had arrived.

Boldly, reminding herself that she had come too far to chicken out now, Kelsey moved forward to join the line. Inside the launch, she chose a seat on the port side, farthest away from *Naiad*. Moments later she stepped ashore, surrounded by excitedly chattering American tourists.

So far, so good. What next?

Kelsey sent a desperate glance around the crowded square. With her blond hair and crimson slacks, she would make an all-too-easy target to spot. From down here in the town, she couldn't even call to alert Michael. The windmill wasn't equipped with one of the island's few telephones.

A nearby conversation intruded on her worried thoughts. 'The assistant purser told me that the only buses here on Mykonos just go back and forth to the airport,' a

Midwesterny voice declared. 'To get out to Paradise Beach, we'll need to take a cab.'

Fervently Kelsey wished she could simply do the same thing. But taxi drivers had a knack of remembering people—and their destinations. By hailing one, she would risk leading the enemy straight to her friends.

Not if she was just part of a group, though, she thought suddenly. As one of hundreds of cruise passengers, she'd be practically invisible.

The four young women who were discussing the beach trip had sat a few seats ahead of her aboard the launch. Kelsey stepped forward and smiled when one of them waved for a cab. 'Would you mind if I rode part of the way with you? That's an awful hike in this heat, but I'm dying to get some close-up photos of those darling windmills up on the ridge.'

'Sure. Hop in and put your money away,' came the friendly order when she reached for her wallet, intending to contribute to the fare. 'We'll be going right past there, anyway. Just show the driver where you want to get off.'

By the time Kelsey stepped away from the working windmill she'd been pretending to take an interest in, the taxi's exhaust was dissipating in the distance. A mere two hundred yards down the slope stood the landmark owned by Stefanos's great-aunt. She'd done it!

In sight of her goal, Kelsey tensed to repress a shudder. Somehow she'd done it—and kept

143

from panicking too, even though she'd been caught almost literally between the devil and the deep-blue sea! But it had been close. So close. Had it not been for a well-placed air vent, they'd have snared her in their nasty trap.

How cunning they were! Too clever to be deceived for long, Kelsey knew. They must have already figured out her escape route. Geoff and the others were sure to be ashore by now, searching. . . .

This time the impulse to look back could not be denied. Still pelting downhill, Kelsey darted a frightened glance toward the road.

And felt a strong pair of hands reach out to grab her arms!

CHAPTER EIGHT

'Easy! Don't be frightened, Kelsey. You weren't watching where you were going. I just didn't want you to fall and hurt yourself again.'

Michael's soothing tone was aimed at calming the agitated young woman he had caught in his arms. 'Last night I saw how you stumbled up the path from the water without giving a thought to how many bruises and scrapes you were collecting. Knowing I was the one who had caused you to run off in such a state made me feel like a real heel. Then a minute ago I stepped outside and there you were, tearing downhill as if one of Mykonos's notorious old-time pirates were about to slit your gizzard.'

Kelsey shivered and began tugging Michael urgently toward the windmill guest house. 'Hurry, please! Get inside and bolt the door before my luck runs out—and yours along with it. Somebody I met today would look perfectly natural with an eye patch and cutlass!'

Even after gaining the safety of the big, round room, Kelsey had a hard time making her teeth stop chattering. She shot an anxious glance around. 'Where's Zoe?'

'Safe. Out in the kitchen, keeping Philomena company. We planned to have an early lunch today,' Michael added, not looking a bit happy about the reason he'd deemed this necessary. 'The ferry is scheduled—'

She gave her head an adamant shake. 'It'll have to leave without me.'

'Kelsey, we've been over this before. I don't want to send you away any more than you want to go. But as I tried to explain last night—'

'It's for my own safety?' Her laugh had a half-hysterical edge to it. 'Too late to worry about that, Michael. Those people know exactly who I am. What had me so terrified was the fear I might be leading them to you and Zoe.'

The news shook Michael, but he didn't flinch, any more than he questioned the truth of what she was saying. He realized that while Kelsey might argue, she would never lie to him. Apology mingled with dejection in his voice. 'I thought I'd been so careful.'

He'd taken every possible precaution, Kelsey knew, but still his efforts seemed to have been in vain. Most people would have admitted defeat and thrown in the sponge by now. She wrapped his right hand in both of hers, repaying the concern he'd earlier shown for her.

'Not even James Bond wins every single skirmish,' she said hearteningly. 'They must have guessed you would return to Seattle after whisking Zoe out of their reach in Florida. Most likely they got lucky. They spotted you entering Joanna's office, then put two and two together because of the type of business she runs. Monitoring the plane reservations she made couldn't have been too difficult. As soon as she booked a flight to Athens for a woman and child, they dispatched an agent to intercept us at London.'

She told him how, seemingly by chance, Sarah Twelvetrees had been assigned the seat next to theirs on the jet.

'It was a huge, wide-bodied plane, with hundreds of people aboard. Sarah gave us one glance, then began staring around. When I asked if she was looking for somebody in particular, she said no, that the art gallery where she works had an important clientele

146

and she didn't want to accidentally overlook anyone. But today I found out that it was really a seven-year-old girl she kept trying to spot.'

Kelsey looked up to meet Michael's eyes. 'Sarah had chalked me off as just another single parent traveling with her little boy. Zoe pulled the wool over her eyes with that Jason disguise.'

'Talk about a lucky break!' he said wonderingly. 'I never dreamed the two of you would be in any danger. And to think I let myself be bamboozled into going off to Ios instead of seeing you safely to your hotel.'

'It's a good thing you fell for their ruse. After all, if you hadn't, you wouldn't have picked up Ione and Rupert's trail or learned how the trunk happened to be left there years ago. But the real silver lining was that if you *had* shown up at the airport, there would have been no doubt about Zoe's identity. Sarah's "gentleman friend," as she called him, would have scooped us all in together. The way it worked out, they were forced to call off your assassination—'

'What!'

Kelsey nodded emphatically. 'Since Zoe had slipped through their fingers again, they couldn't afford to let Nico shoot you.' She should have felt surprised that the sniper's name leaped so easily to her lips, but Kelsey had a feeling that she would never forget a single word of that sinister conversation she'd

147

overheard from the 'loo' aboard *Naiad*. 'Geoff appears to be Mr Van Ryn's right-hand man as well as Sarah's boyfriend. He tagged along when he failed to interfere with your catching the ferry and managed to shove you out of the bullet's way, even though he had to elbow a path through a herd of goats to do so.'

'Serves him right!' Michael was scowling over a name she'd mentioned. 'Nobody knows a whole lot about Huntley Van Ryn except that he's a billionaire several times over—and so keen on privacy he makes Howard Hughes sound gregarious by comparison. But why would he be mixed up in anything this shady? He owns an entire island down in the Caribbean, and it's rumored that not even the Louvre has an art collection to rival his.'

'We're definitely talking about the same man then. In *Naiad*'s salon I noticed a pair of original oils that could easily have been Rembrandts. There was also a small statue on an end table too exquisite to have been sculpted by anyone except Michelangelo.'

'Listen, Kelsey, I think you'd better tell me how you became involved with these people and their ritzy yacht in the first place. This morning I asked Zoe to let you sleep late, knowing you had a long trip ahead of you. I figured it would be more comfortable for everyone that way. Especially since you weren't even talking to me any longer.'

She flushed, recalling her anger of the

evening before. Michael's decision to send her away had seemed miserably unfair, particularly since his actions had seemed to indicate that he was beginning to care for her very much.

'Sometimes I have a hard time listening to reason,' she admitted. 'This morning I felt wretched for having acted like such a brat. I would have told you so, except that when I woke up, you had already gone out. So I decided to use my last few hours in Greece taking a look at Mykonos and buying some gifts to bring home to my family.'

She described her walk down to the waterfront, where she had noticed the yacht, then watched the *Golden Odyssey* approach. After buying her tiles, she had encountered Sarah and foolishly allowed herself to be lured out to *Naiad*. Thanks to more than one stroke of good fortune, she had learned who it was she'd become mixed up with and made her escape.

'I doubt I could ever have gotten away if it weren't for the cruise ship. Lucky for me that's a shallow harbor and the passengers had to be taken ashore by launch. I rode into port with them, then hitched a ride up the hill with a taxiload of tourists heading toward Paradise Beach.'

Kelsey sighed, thinking of the box of ceramic tiles she'd been forced to abandon. 'Earlier, the thought crossed my mind that the cats I saw prowling around those twisting alleys were the only freebooters left on the island nowadays. How could I have been so wrong? This Huntley Van Ryn sounds like the sort of man who wouldn't hesitate to make someone walk the plank, if that was the only way he could get his hands on something he wanted.'

Michael had heard about other rich collectors who would literally kill to obtain a rare art treasure. 'They feel their money entitles them to have it all. And you can believe that the objects they acquire through their Machiavellian schemes are never lent to a museum or gallery for the rest of the world to enjoy. Priceless items just seem to disappear off the face of the earth.'

'I wouldn't be surprised if that's how Sarah became involved with those two,' Kelsey said. 'She mentioned spending time in the West Indies because her gallery has a branch in Antigua. Huntley Van Ryn might have encountered her there, commissioned her to locate additions for his exclusive collection. I'll bet she was the one who turned up those bits of Etruscan jewelry that Paul Durer sold to pay for his passage to Greece.' A small smile tugged at her lips. 'If so, it explains why they put up with her passion for shopping till she drops. Geoff looked mighty disgruntled when he saw that armload of packages she carted back to the yacht this morning.'

'Stupidity would be a far more serious weakness than acquisitiveness, from Van Ryn's point of view. No matter how valuable her finds have been in the past, she'll be lucky to escape from this latest blunder with her skin intact,' Michael predicted.

Kelsey knew he must be thinking of the fate that befell Alec Westerlin. Despite Sarah's attempts to lure her into a trap, she hoped that the Englishwoman would not be the next person to be struck down by a hit-and-run driver.

'I know,' she agreed uncomfortably. 'She's botched it twice now, hasn't she?'

'Yeah. A few days ago she was taken in by a disguise thought up by a seven-year-old. This morning, instead of sticking as close to you as your own shadow, she let you slip through their net again.'

Michael's direct gaze fastened on Kelsey. 'We're both still here because of that woman's ineptitude, but we don't dare count on getting any more unintentional help. From now on neither of us is going to make a move the other doesn't know about. We're going to be a team, you and I. Somehow, working together, we'll see this thing through.'

Tears of relief sprang to Kelsey's eyes. Though leveling with her about the danger, Michael was also admitting that he needed her help. By trusting her, depending on her, he was placing his life in her hands.

Never had she felt more highly complimented. There were things she wanted to say, promises she yearned to make. Fortunately, since there was no guarantee she'd have the ability to carry them through, Zoe chose that moment to come dancing into the room.

Her close-cropped hair was a mass of ringlets. Even in roughneck play she looked dainty and entirely feminine. Thank heaven she had slept the whole way from London to Athens, Kelsey thought. Not even someone as dense as Sarah would have been deceived for long, with 'Jason' alert and chattering.

Unceremoniously the little girl made room for herself between the two adults. 'Hi, Kelsey. I'm glad you're back. I hope you changed your mind about going away and leaving us.'

'Yes. Yes, I sure did.' Kelsey was unable to keep a quaver of emotion out of her voice. It was Michael who had changed his mind about allowing her to stay and help, but the end result was the same. She wouldn't be leaving Greece, after all. Not as long as she was needed. Quickly she changed the subject. 'Did you have an interesting time this morning?'

Zoe bobbed her head. 'Uh-huh. I'm sorry you weren't up in time to come along. You would have liked those real old pictures Dr Youvis showed us.'

'Frescoes,' her uncle supplied the proper term.

'That's right. *Fres*-coes.' Zoe bounced around on the sofa. 'You know why the frescoes didn't get ruined by the ocean, Kelsey? 'Cuz for three and a half thousand years they were all covered up tight by lava and ash that 'sploded out of a volcano. And you know something else?'

'No. Tell me.'

'The place where that volcano is used to be a great big round island. Now it's just teeny. There were some other islands, too, that floated on top of the sea for people to live on. They sank, too, or parts of them did.' The little girl's eyes were round and shiny with excitement. 'That's what my mom must have meant, Kelsey, 'bout drawing the maps with her mind's eye. She added in those places that disappeared under the water, just like they were still up on top where everyone could see them.'

So that was why the islands on Ione's charts had appeared to be 'crowdeder together'!

Kelsey was used to working with intelligent youngsters whose imaginations were often captivated by concepts too mature for their understanding. Part of her job was to help them separate fact from embroidery, without spoiling the zest for learning new things. But here, the reality of the event that had changed the configuration of the Aegean forever was so monumental, it was almost impossible to exaggerate its effects. What's more, a major cataclysm occurring that far back in history would have been a familiar topic to a professor of classical studies such as Ione Devos Strasse.

'Wow!' she exclaimed. 'That's really an exciting adventure tale. Do you know the name of the island that blew apart?'

Zoe nodded in delight. She loved stories, all kinds. Two of her current favorites were about a wooden puppet who turned into a real boy, and a barnyard spider who spun words into her webs to help a friend. At seven Zoe was old enough to know that Pinocchio and Charlotte were make-believe characters. But just now she'd been talking about something real. It pleased her that Kelsey had termed it an 'adventure tale' instead of just a 'story.' Someday her own real-life job would have to do with adventures too. Digging up wonderful things like those *fres*-coes and learning more about the people who had lived so long ago.

'Yes,' she cried excitedly. 'It was called Santorini!'

*   *   *

For centuries, Kelsey knew, scholars had been debating about whether Santorini—now often called Thira, or Thera—was or was not the 'lost city' of Atlantis. A confusing amount of evidence seemed to support both sides of the issue. Whether it had once been home to a superior civilization wasn't her concern just now, however. All through lunch, which Philomena came in to announce while Zoe's revelation was still ringing in the air, she kept trying to puzzle out something else. What connection could sunken islands have with the quest that had brought them all to Greece? After all, the place where Paul Duval had spent the final few weeks of his life still existed.

On the other hand, she reminded herself, that trunk had been empty when he bartered it for board and room. The old man must have disposed of its contents before ever arriving on Ios.

Zoe was tuckered out by the morning's activities. Yawns overtook her in the middle of the meal. Cassandra coaxed her into having another sip of lemonade, then led her upstairs to lie down.

Michael sent a sympathetic glance after his niece as her short legs trudged up the spiral staircase. 'Poor little kid. She must have felt a lot like Atlas, balancing the weight of the whole world on her shoulders. I hadn't realized how much that remark of Ione's bothered her until we finally figured out what it meant.'

'About drawing things from her mind's eye? Yes, that was a pretty mysterious puzzle for a child to unravel. After you left Seattle, she had a terrible struggle with her conscience,' Kelsey confided. 'Her dad had warned her not to talk about anything she'd seen or heard during their family conferences. Zoe kept trying to

155

decide whether that ban should extend to you, as well as to everybody else. Then she remembered Rupert had promised they would be gone only a little while, and she got to fretting that her parents might be in serious trouble.'

'Her decision to speak up turned out to be mighty important. Suggesting that the islands in Ione's drawings were larger and more numerous than the way they appear on actual charts gave me a new angle to explore,' Michael said. 'As well as the "digs" he participates in, Dr Youvis is also a noted authority on myth. I hoped he could help me locate a shrine that had existed someplace off the beaten path, yet not too far from Ios. Because of Zoe's input, it also occurred to me to ask whether the site would still be accessible.'

From the look of suppressed excitement on Michael's face, Kelsey guessed that the archaeologist had been able to furnish him with a vital clue. 'What did he say?'

'That there *was* a place sacred to Aphrodite located about a dozen miles southeast of Ios. It's mostly under water at the moment.'

A frown creased Kelsey's brow. 'I don't understand. How can that information be of value? If those islands sank thousands of years ago—'

'They didn't—not all of them,' Michael hastily explained. 'That massive explosion

Plato wrote about, the one that ripped Santorini apart and practically buried Crete under mountains of debris, took place around 1500 B.C.'

Dr Youvis had told him that modern historians were beginning to connect other incidents of the same time period to that tremendous cataclysm. Some scholars contended that the dramatic events chronicled in the Bible's book of Exodus, such as the parting of the Red Sea and the series of plagues visited on Egypt, could logically have resulted from the same catastrophe.

'It was the most violent natural disaster the world has ever witnessed, but not the only one to strike this region, by a long shot,' Michael said. 'At least two of the Seven Wonders of the Ancient World were destroyed by other earthquakes. The countries rimming the Mediterranean are at least as seismic-prone as our own West Coast is.'

Volcanoes, Kelsey knew, had a lot to do with earthquakes. That was what the term 'Ring of Fire' referred to. But tremblers could also rock areas a long way from a smoldering crater. San Francisco's devastating quakes of 1906 and 1989 gave tragic proof of this.

'So you're telling me that this place where people once honored Aphrodite didn't sink all that long ago?'

'Santorini's volcano, Nea Kameni, started causing problems again in the middle of the

1800s,' Michael confirmed this assumption. 'It erupted in 1925, and is still a long way from dormant. In June of 1956 a terrible earthquake knocked about two thousand of the island's houses into the sea. That same rumble also affected a number of nearby islands. Thalassos was one that happened to. All but its mountainous tip sank beneath the surface.'

'Thalassos?' The name was unfamiliar to Kelsey. 'Is that the island where Dr Youvis said the ancient shrine was located?'

Michael nodded. 'Back in the days before Socrates, believers would make pilgrimages there. Aphrodite was the goddess of love, you know. I imagine a lot of petitions got sent her way. However, for the past five centuries the local residents have done an excellent job of keeping the place a secret.'

In 1537, he went on, the Ottoman ruler of Turkey, Süleyman the Magnificent, seized control of Santorini. With the Turkish invaders established only a few miles south of their own rocky little island, the entire population of Thalassos agreed on a pact to conceal the venerable old sanctuary.

'They didn't trust the Turks, to say the least. The local folks found a way to seal off the entrance to the hillside cave where the shrine was located, hoping that would protect the beautiful life-sized statue of Aphrodite from being carried away.'

'Very wise, considering what happened at

the Parthenon,' Kelsey commented. 'Michael, could Ione have obtained this same piece of information from Dr Youvis?'

'No, because she never came here to Mykonos. I checked. But other antiquarians would have known of the shrine. People like the classicists at the monasteries. I imagine that's where Paul Duval learned about Thalassos. Having him, as well as Ione and Rupert, show up on Ios makes me certain they were all following the same lead.'

The timing would certainly have worked, Kelsey mused. The old man had begun his long journey from Germany early in 1950. Upon arrival, he'd spent months traveling around the Greek mainland, hauling his oversized piece of baggage in a mule cart. Then, only weeks before his death, he had come to Ios. With an empty trunk.

'Paul Duval could really have accomplished what he set out to do,' she said. 'That last big earthquake didn't cause Thalassos to sink until six years after his death.'

'Right,' Michael agreed. 'What with the shrine having been sealed up for five centuries, it had probably been all but forgotten even by what was left of the local population. If the goatherds noticed him at all, they wouldn't have paid much attention to an elderly man wandering around the hillsides.'

'So the treasure would still be there!'

'Provided he ever had it. There's never been

a shred of proof that he smuggled the Trojan gold out of Germany and into Greece,' Michael put a rein on Kelsey's enthusiasm. 'But yes. *If* it was Priam's treasure he was hauling around in the trunk, it's a good bet that shrine is where he would have stashed it.'

'It would be strange if Ione and Rupert hadn't followed up on those clues—gone to Thalassos themselves.'

'Not strange. Unthinkable. What's worrying me,' Michael said, 'is why they've never returned.'

* * *

Almost positive now of the missing couple's destination, a feeling of urgency overtook them both. With Stefanos off somewhere beyond Rhodes in the seaplane, their only means of transportation was the sturdy fishing vessel he'd left behind. The water journey would be far slower than going by air. This made it all the more imperative that they leave at the earliest possible moment.

'But not with Zoe,' Michael stipulated. 'I'm almost afraid to think about what we might find on Thalassos. If something terrible has happened to my sister and brother-in-law, I don't want their daughter along to see it with her own eyes. If necessary, you and I can try to soften the blow for her later.'

Zoe's safety was an equally important

160

consideration. They decided to take her to stay with a married cousin of Stefanos. Maria had a large family; one more child would go unnoticed among the rollicking crowd of youngsters. This plan was arranged and carried out that very afternoon, though not without protest by the individual most concerned.

'*Why* can't I come with you, Uncle Michael?'

'Because I have decided it wouldn't be a good idea.' His good-bye hug was affectionate, but his tone said the decision was final. 'We'll be back before you know it.'

'That's what my daddy said too.' Big, glistening tears beaded in Zoe's eyes, making it hard for Kelsey to keep her own lip from wobbling. She felt that Michael was right about leaving Zoe behind, though, and liked the way Maria and Andreas, the children, and their live-in grandparents absorbed the morose little girl into the household.

Among the supplies aboard the fishing boat were canvas tarps, coils of new rope, and extra fuel for the engine. To these Michael added an additional armload of blankets and an up-to-date first-aid kit, passing them down to Kelsey, who stowed them in the space below decks. Bunks and a compact galley were among the tidily arranged facilities there.

'The fresh-water tank is full, and there's a minimum supply of food,' she reported, climbing back up to join him in the wheelhouse. 'Enough to feed four people, say, for a couple of days.'

'That should be plenty. If all goes well, we'll be back here within twenty-four hours.'

Nevertheless, Michael added to the larder. He stowed tea, pasta, beans, and dried fruit in the galley cupboards and left a fistful of drachmas with Philomena to pay for the supplies he had appropriated.

The first wisps of dawn were threading a gossamer web across the eastern sky when he and Kelsey picked their way down the cliff to the boat's snug berth the next morning. With no show of lights and a minimum of noise, they put out from shore. Farther down, the town lay dark and silent. Clad in a dark-ribbed turtleneck, Michael gestured toward the quiet scene.

'Mykonos just fell into bed about the time we were getting up. Let's hope the group aboard *Naiad* keeps late hours also.'

'Is that why we didn't leave last night?'

Shaking his head, he pointed to a patch of foam a few yards off their starboard bow. Looking more closely, Kelsey saw that the endless ribbons of bubbles didn't quite mask a jagged outcrop of rock.

'That one's marked on the chart, but a lot of hazards aren't,' Michael said. 'Even in daylight, navigation through these waters is no piece of cake. Want to take the wheel?'

'Of course.'

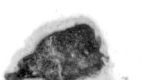

Kelsey realized the invitation was a test, a serious one. Undaunted, she stepped forward. She had asked to be a partner in this venture; it was her intention to be a full-fledged one.

Efficiently noting the compass reading, she changed places with Michael. Kelsey was very glad now that she'd taken the time to braid her long blond hair and pin it securely to the back of her neck. With reefs and shoals to watch for, she didn't need anything blowing in her eyes.

Michael stood nearby, closely observing her seamanship for a quarter of an hour. Then he nodded in satisfaction. Turning, he reached toward the rack where an array of tackle had been neatly stowed. Instead of pulling out one of the fishing poles, however, his hand closed over the edge of the wooden frame. Kelsey's eyes widened as the plywood-backed rack swung open, revealing a tall but narrow hidey-hole notched into the bulkhead. Inside, a faint sheen of light flooded across the barrel of a high-powered rifle.

'Ah,' she said, 'so that's what Stefanos meant by referring to extra supplies that might come in handy. Somehow I didn't think he meant just groceries.'

'No.' A look of amusement flickered briefly across Michael's face. Unstrapping the rifle, he raised it to his shoulder, squinting through the sights as he aimed across the empty water. The barest squeeze of his finger sent a noisy fusillade spurting harmlessly into space. His expression had grown completely serious by the time he'd examined the rest of the concealed arsenal, test-fired a pair of handguns, then reloaded every empty chamber and replaced the artillery where it belonged.

He seemed to find it hard to tell what she was thinking. 'Sometimes,' he commented quietly, 'it becomes necessary to fight fire with fire. I was glad that while I was in the Navy, there was never any need to go into combat. But I wouldn't have hesitated to do so, had my country been in jeopardy. I feel the same way about defending the people who are dear to me. Do you shoot as well as you handle a boat?'

Kelsey shook her head. 'Not nearly. The idea of killing things never appealed to me.'

'Could you, if it was essential?'

She had a good eye. Could she aim at a person instead of a paper target and squeeze off an accurate shot? Kelsey believed she could, if Michael's life were on the line. Or Zoe's. Or, she supposed, her own. She lifted her eyes to meet his steady gaze. 'Yes. If there was absolutely no other alternative.'

'Good.' Remarking that harpoons and a flare gun were included in Stefanos's arsenal, he pulled open a compartment beneath a bench and showed her a lethal-looking assortment of knives concealed by fishnets. 'Weapons aplenty if we need them, and I pray we won't. There's also a good pair of binoculars here in the drawer. We'll take turns keeping watch for *Naiad*.'

Kelsey had hoped that was one hazard they'd left completely behind. Now she shot a glance over her shoulder to reassure herself that nowhere on the horizon was there any sign of another vessel. 'We aren't being followed. Heavens, they don't even know we have a boat. How could they possibly anticipate where we'd be headed?'

'I'm hoping they can't, but I wouldn't want to bet our lives on it,' Michael said reasonably. 'With Van Ryn's money he could hire a platoon of hit men or send an armada after us, if he was so inclined. I don't believe he'll do that. The more people involved, the more rumors later. Even he can arrange just so many hit-and-run accidents.'

The stakes were too high to risk an investigation, Kelsey agreed. 'At least three governments would jump in to squabble over possession if word leaked out that he—or anyone—had discovered the missing Trojan treasure.'

'Which doesn't mean he won't track us with every resource at his command. Just that it will be done discreetly,' Michael warned, then muffled a sigh. 'I'd give anything, Kelsey, if you were safely on the other side of the world instead of here, in harm's way. I'm almost positive I'd like to spend the rest of my life being your husband, but so far there's been no chance even to explore how we feel about each other. I'm not about to ask a woman to marry me when half my time is spent dodging bullets.'

Kelsey felt the breath jam in her throat. As a non-proposal, that was a stunner. She didn't need to ask herself how she felt about him. Looking back, she suspected that she had fallen in love with Michael Devos the moment he walked through the door of her apartment, clinging supportively to the hand of his small niece. He was a loyal, loving, utterly marvelous man. Being his wife—if he ever asked her— would be the pinnacle of all her dreams.

'You—you've only had to dodge them once,' she pointed out shakily.

'So far.'

'One of the bad guys even knocked you out of the line of fire.'

'Not because he liked me. I'm hoping you feel differently.' Stepping closer, Michael reached up and smoothed a wisp of hair back from her brow. 'In case we ever find a minute to stop running, you might want to be deciding on an answer.'

'That won't be hard. If I'm called on to provide it, of course.'

Relieved brown eyes met starry blue ones. 'Count on it!'

*   *   *

Every half hour, as they made their way due

south across an oddly glassy sea, Michael tuned the fishing boat's shortwave radio to a news and weather station. The Greek language announcements were too rapid-fire for Kelsey even to begin to understand, but two words, repeated several times on the nine-thirty broadcast, caught her attention.

'Nea Kameni? Is he talking about Santorini's volcano?'

Michael nodded. He continued to listen intently until the bulletin ended. By the time he snapped off the dial, his expression had grown extremely troubled.

'The volcano is rumbling again. An eruption doesn't seem to be imminent, but seismologists are concerned about quakes. They're warning the people on Thera, Santorini's main town, to be prepared for sizable tremors.'

Great, Kelsey thought. That would be all they needed. Particularly since their own destination lay about halfway between Santorini and Ios. A major, modern-day earthquake had already caused most of Thalassos to submerge. Another one—

'What about the rest of the area?' she asked quickly, worrying as much for Ione and Rupert as for themselves.

'Anything might happen. Or nothing.' Michael tried coaxing a few more knots of speed out of the boat's engine.

Despite the push for speed he was a careful navigator, double-checking their position whenever they came within sight of an island, then marking the charts with small, neat x's. By the time they maneuvered through the channel dividing Paros from Naxos to the east, the sun was riding high in the cloudless sky. Kelsey made a quick trip belowdecks to change into lighter-weight clothing. Michael peeled off his heavy turtleneck. The close-fitting white T-shirt he wore underneath emphasized his well-muscled physique and made a striking contrast against his olive skin.

He grew progressively quieter as the hours passed. Concern over what lay ahead had crowded out all other considerations now, Kelsey knew. When he pointed to a hazy spot of land, remarking that Ios lay off their port beam, she decided that it would be a good time to have something to eat. Later they might be too busy to think about food.

'How about lunch?' she suggested. 'If you'll take the wheel, I'll see what I can rustle up.'

'Fine.' Michael changed places with her, consulted the charts, and made a degree's alteration in the compass heading. As she went below, Kelsey wished the ordeal were over. Waiting and worrying—those were the hardest things to do.

They ate standing up, seldom relaxing their vigilance, even though the mugs of tea and hearty cheese sandwiches eased a little of the tension. To Kelsey, it seemed odd that they had encountered so few pleasure boats on such a beautiful summer day. Even fishermen plying their nets had been all but nonexistent. The uneasy notion came to her that other skippers might be staying in port because of the ominous forecast.

There was one major advantage to having the Aegean to themselves. It meant that *Naiad* and her murderous crew were far away.

Half an hour later Michael abruptly slackened speed. He handed Kelsey the binoculars, which had been dangling around his own neck.

'That hump of land ahead is what remains of Thalassos. From now on we'll need to keep a mighty sharp lookout. We're going to be sailing on top of a partially submerged island. How *far* submerged is anybody's guess. The fathoms of water under our keel are sure to vary constantly.' Only the central peak was currently visible, he added, but the island's entire landscape had been ruggedly mountainous. Other crags were likely to be lurking just below the surface.

In Kelsey's view, Thalassos had little to offer that would make a person want to stay and explore. The brown, barren earth that became more fully discernible as the boat drew closer was thinly covered by patches of grass so parched that not even a goat would be tempted to nibble. If at one time the island's economy had included olive groves or other crops, no sign of this growth remained. She found it hard

169

to believe that pilgrims had once journeyed to this sere, isolated place, seeking Aphrodite's blessing for an affair of the heart.

Then Kelsey glanced back at Michael and decided that maybe it wasn't so hard to believe, after all.

After that, what little she was able to see of Thalassos was garnered from quick, darting glimpses. Her job was to stare alertly down into the water, keeping her eyes open for concealed hazards. Standing at the boat's prow while it chugged ahead at a dog-paddle dawdle, she used hand signals to warn Michael away from snags that might foul their propeller or rip a hole in the keel. Twice peaks wavering just beneath the surface closed in on three sides. While both of them held their breath, Michael put the engine into reverse and backed slowly to a safer position.

As the minutes passed, Kelsey felt her spirits drooping. Logic declared that this was the place where Ione and Rupert were most likely to be found, yet as they circled the island from as close in as they were able to get, there had been no sign of life. No indication that any living being except sea birds had visited this dead island in decades.

Staring down into the wavery depths, Kelsey blinked as an inlet opened ahead and the reflection of something pale came into view. Simultaneously she heard a sharp intake of breath from the man behind her.

'Oh, no!' Michael groaned. 'I was afraid something like that might have happened!'

CHAPTER NINE

Reluctant to look, yet knowing there was no choice, Kelsey raised her head to stare at the shoreline scene fifty yards ahead. You couldn't call it a beach, she thought. Not really. Just a high plateau with water lapping at its edges.

The mirror image she'd spied wavering in the water had been the reflection of a boat. Now, stern-on, she saw it directly. Details leaped at her—more grayish than white; fair-sized but scruffy looking; bleached-out canvas top and peeling paint. Then their own boat shifted. She caught a new angle and saw what had torn that agitated cry from Michael. The motorboat had been dragged half out of the water. Someone—sometime—had made a not-very-professional attempt to patch a gaping hole in its bow.

The splintered damage was a stark reminder of their own precarious position. Kelsey jerked her gaze back from the grounded vessel to peer anxiously down into the shallows. In a series of ripples the odd, distorted reflection of the fishing boat's hull undulated back at her. Ahead, strangely, the water didn't swirl. It looked rigid. Immobile.

Solid.

'Michael, stop! Don't go any farther!'

The fact that he'd been proceeding at a dead-slow pace averted disaster. Instantaneously he cut the engine, then peered forward to assess the obstacle Kelsey had spotted.

'It's an underwater hillside!' he exclaimed.

With extreme caution he restarted the engine. Guiding the boat in reverse, Michael retreated an inch, a foot, a yard, two. The bottom receded. Shallows deepened. Water, sunlit and reassuringly liquid, swirled ahead of them once again.

Breath expelled in two audible gusts of relief. But when the anchor was down, preventing them from drifting ahead, the earlier crisis still remained to be dealt with.

Michael's jaw tightened as he unbuckled his wrist-watch. Kelsey bent over and started to loosen the strap of her sandal. He caught her hand, stilling the motion.

'No. Stay here. Please?'

Unwillingly she straightened up again, yearning to argue, to plead, to insist on going ashore with him, to lend as much assistance as she could. But the stark expression on his face let her know that having her along would only make the ordeal harder for him. People he loved had been shipwrecked here on Thalassos. Their survival was in doubt, to say the least. During the passage from Mykonos, Michael had steeled himself to cope with whatever would have to be handled. His eyes told her he couldn't do it as unflinchingly if she were on the spot, sharing in his misery.

All she had left to offer was moral support. 'Aye-aye, captain. I'll be right here if you need me.'

Michael gave her fingers a grateful squeeze, then closed them around his watch. But before he could turn to dive over the side, an urgent shout stunned them both.

'Ahoy!'

At first sight the beached motorboat had appeared to be abandoned. Now it gave an unsteady lurch as a raggedly bearded man emerged from below decks.

'Ahoy, yourself!' Michael's answering shout sounded exuberant. 'Rupert, that's your voice, but I sure don't recognize the face!'

From shore echoed a chagrined laugh. 'I'm not surprised. Shaving's been a bit difficult lately, what with one thing and another. Because of the water shortage, my wife decided she could tolerate the beard if I could stand the way it itched.'

'Wife?' Seeing the sudden pallor of the handsome young man at her side, Kelsey felt certain that until this very moment he had been convinced that Ione must be dead. He leaned forward, a question hovering on his lips.

Rupert's anxious warning forestalled it. 'Listen, you don't dare stay where you are! Once it starts to turn, the tide literally peels away from this shore. Everything gets swept along in its wake. There's a nasty reef not too far out. You'll be flung up against it if you don't get away in a hurry!'

The motorboat seesawed. With agonizingly careful steps, Rupert edged nearer the rail. For the first time Kelsey noticed the makeshift sling binding his right arm flat against his chest.

'Michael, he's been hurt!'

'Yeah, and he doesn't look strong enough to endure much of a swim. If we leave here, how are we ever going to get him—them—aboard?'

That point had been worrying Kelsey too. That and the question of Ione. Where was she? Rupert's agitation was too marked to be ignored, however. Frantically he pointed to the left.

'Over there, the other side of Zeus's Marbles, lies a good, safe anchorage. Deep and sheltered. It's the island's original harbor. We put in there on our first visit. Things would be different if we could have made it that far the second time. Get out of here, Michael! Hurry!'

In just the short time since they'd spotted the wreck, the churning surf had receded from beneath the motorboat. Water was pulling away from land like a drink being sucked through a straw. Michael made a dash for the wheelhouse. The engine sputtered to life while the anchor chain was still clanking upward.

Kelsey's dumbfounded gaze was trapped by the formation Rupert had referred to as Zeus's

Marbles. The name seemed awesomely appropriate. Dozens of gigantic boulders looked as if they had been gouged out of the earth, then flung into a high, haphazard heap by some powerful being who reveled in violent games. They completely blocked the view to the east, but raw scars indicated that they hadn't always been piled atop one another.

With a shiver she realized that the most recent earthquake must have been what caused the boulders' upheaval. It must have been a terrifying experience for the people living here on Thalassos, watching their island being ripped apart before their very eyes. She wondered what had happened to Aphrodite's ancient shrine during the cataclysm. The cave could have tumbled into a crevasse—

'Kelsey! Hold on!'

Michael's desperate shout roused her to danger. The outgoing tide had begun exerting a pull that dragged them backward at a dizzy speed. While he manhandled the boat into a jolting U-turn, she shoved his watch into her pocket, then grabbed for the railing with both hands.

The next six or seven minutes passed in a frenzied blur. White water lashed their bow, cascading torrents of drenching spray into the air. Within seconds Kelsey was soaked, the decks awash. She felt like a rider without a seat belt, trying to shoot the rapids of the Snake River aboard a careening roller coaster.

Vicious crosscurrents battered the boat's hull. She was dreadfully aware that back there in the wheelhouse Michael must be exerting every ounce of strength in an effort to force the boat laterally along the coast. The alternative was certain death: If the tide had its way, they would be funneled back into the jagged reef lying in wait offshore. Kelsey caught horrifying glimpses of toothed, shiny black rocks spurting geysers of frothing surf back at the sea. Then the boat was spinning in circles and all she could think of was Michael.

Hold on . . . Please, God, let him hold on!

Suddenly the once-implacable current released its grip. The frightful noise diminished as the fishing boat was all but catapulted into a wide, protective harbor. Beneath Kelsey's feet the heaving deck shuddered, then bobbed to a gradual standstill.

Salt water streamed from her face and clothing as she lifted her head, staring almost in disbelief at the safe haven they had gained. It seemed like a miracle. The surrounding waters were calm, their sapphire depths unruffled. She saw that Zeus's Marbles now lay to the port side of their boat, rather than to starboard, balancing atop one another like huge, grotesquely misshapen cannonballs.

The anchor plunged down with a splash. Urgent footsteps tattooed across the deck. Kelsey pried trembling fingers away from the wooden rail they'd been locked around for so long and spun to throw herself into Michael's arms.

'We're both still alive!'

'Thank God you were able to hold on!'

'Michael, you were wonderful! That ride had me terrified, but the way you wrestled that wheel—'

'Sweetheart, I was scared stiff. But you— you stood up there like a glorious Viking figurehead, defying the elements.' Michael cradled Kelsey's head against his shoulder, running his fingers through her loosened wet braids. 'So long as I could see you there safe, I knew we'd be all right. But if the tide had carried you away—'

'It didn't. I fastened my thoughts on you, praying you'd have the strength to see us through.'

A great sigh of thanksgiving shuddered through Michael. 'It took both of us. We won that battle together. Sweetheart, would you agree to make it a lifetime partnership? I love you so much Kelsey, I'm not just asking, I'm begging. Please. Tell me you'll marry me.'

'Oh, Michael!' Kelsey felt a tug at her heartstrings when she saw that his lashes were damp with emotion. She was crying too, out of relief that they'd both been spared, and for pure, utter joy. The man she adored was going to be her husband!

'I've known for ages that I loved everything about you, but I didn't dare admit it,' he said. 'I kept warning myself that what was between us wasn't personal, that it was only for the sake of Zoe—'

Awareness of the rest of the world surged back to intrude on their moment of sweet togetherness. On Mykonos a child was waiting for them to locate her parents. Here, on Thalassos, Rupert, at least, was alive, depending on them to bring him safely home.

'Yes, Michael darling. To answer your question, yes, yes, yes!' Kelsey wrapped her arms around his neck. Her kiss promised everything there was no time to say in words. Then she fished his waterlogged watch out of her pocket and handed it over with a rueful grimace.

'Too bad this isn't one of those things that takes a licking and keeps on ticking. But even though it's stopped, I guess we'd better not waste any more time in finishing what we came to do.'

'Right. Let's get moving. Your future in-laws must be thoroughly sick of this island by now.'

From one of the deck lockers, Michael unearthed a rope ladder. While he secured it to the boat's side, letting the ends dangle below the surface to make it easy to climb aboard again, Kelsey ran below and filled a thermos with fresh water. She also wrapped the dried fruit in a waterproof pouch, then stuffed both items into a string bag to be slipped over her wrist as she swam.

'Rupert mentioned a water shortage,' she explained as the two of them let themselves down into the bay's warm waters. 'They've probably been rationing out their food very carefully too.'

Wading ashore, Michael commented that Thalassos was the most inhospitable-looking place he'd ever encountered. Kelsey knew he must be stewing over why Ione hadn't shown up there on the motorboat's deck beside Rupert. The sooner they learned the answers, the better for everyone's morale. At once she led the way toward the precariously balanced heap of boulders.

Finding a gap to slip through was not as difficult as she had at first feared. One of the rocks seemed to sway as her arm brushed its rough surface. Looking up, she saw that it was not quite resting against the slope of the cliff. Then, to their relief, they were past the ponderous barrier.

On the opposite side of Zeus's Marbles, she and Michael both came to an astonished standstill. In a very short time radical changes had taken place in the landscape.

'My gosh!' For many, many yards out, the seawater had been drained completely away, leaving the slick, rugged hillside exposed, and the 'beached' motorboat teeter-tottering at the top of the wetlands. 'It looks like someone yanked the plug out of the bathtub!'

'I'm sure glad Rupert managed to warn us in time,' Michael said feelingly. 'And that the tide was going out instead of flooding in. Can you imagine trying to battle backward against a force like that?'

In spite of the day's warmth, Kelsey felt goose bumps pop out on her skin. From what Rupert had said about not being able to make it around to the safe harbor, she felt certain that was how he had come to be marooned.

Seeing the angle at which the motorboat was listing, she could only marvel at the endurance and determination Zoe's parents must have expended in hauling that cumbersome vessel as far up the slope as they'd managed. A rope had been looped through a bow cleat, then knotted around a large boulder farther up the incline. That was probably all that kept the boat from slithering backward when the tide spurted out from underneath it.

She shivered at the notion of trying to climb down that steeply tilted ladder to the lower deck, with the boat swaying at every motion. And every time the tide went out, it must have been like preparing to go over Niagara Falls in a barrel!

But miraculously both Ione and Rupert had survived. A dark-haired woman waved and gave a glad cry at the sight of them. With an answering whoop, Michael thundered downhill to swing Ione around in a brotherly bear hug.

'You had us worried sick!' he was exclaiming when Kelsey ran forward to join the close-knit group. He drew her forward, introducing her as his wife-to-be, then tried to lighten the emotional moment with a joke. 'We came all this way to fetch you guys so you could dance at our wedding, and what happens? You send Rupert up top alone to tell us to get the heck out of here!'

'I even had to shout at you to make you go!' Rupert stuck out his left hand to clasp Michael's. 'What a feat of seamanship you displayed! The Navy would have been proud of you, brother.'

'Maybe, but Papa would have expected any well-brought-up son of a sponge fisherman to get out of a tight spot occasionally.' People showed their feelings in Michael's family. To cover his emotion and relief at finding his sister and brother-in-law safe, he lifted the string bag off Kelsey's wrist. 'And Mama would say you never visit without bringing a little something. Here you go. Hostess gifts.'

And more than welcome, Kelsey could see. Confessing that they were down to the last few cups in the boat's water tank, Ione insisted on passing the thermos first to her husband. 'I know you've been skimping on your share to leave more for me,' she added, urging him to take a long, refreshing swallow.

Most of the water and the dried apricots, too, disappeared while the Strasses told

181

Michael and Kelsey what had happened. Locating the trunk in Ios and learning that Paul Duval was buried on that island furnished full confirmation of their belief that he'd come to this part of the Aegean to visit Aphrodite's shrine.

'He must have wanted to get as far as he could from Thalassos afterward, for fear of somebody one day following his trail, but he was too ill to go any farther than Ios. Luckily the woman who owned the *taverna* made his last days as comfortable as possible.'

Ione held the thermos up for her husband to have another drink, then continued with the tale. On Ios they had rented a boat to make the journey down to Thalassos. 'We wanted to see how the land lay, decide if there was any chance to discover what we'd come for. But we realized it would be too easy to trace the boat, so we stayed here only a few hours, then returned it to its owner.'

From there they had gone on to Crete, eighty miles to the south, and there managed to pick up an old but reasonably seaworthy motorboat for cash and no questions. But their second trip to Thalassos had met with misfortune. Their boat was caught in the raging floodtide and hurled ashore. Rupert was injured in the violent impact. Despite this, he and Ione had worked together to secure their battered vessel, making a desperate effort to keep it from being dragged back out to sea when the tide turned a few hours later.

'When we heard the sound of your engine half an hour ago, I stayed below to steady our boat while Rupert ran up to warn you about the tide,' Ione explained her earlier mysterious absence. 'If we'd both run up to shout at you, it would have been just our luck to tilt the tottery thing clear over on its side.'

With an arm around each of the women, Michael moved over to take a closer look at the motorboat's damaged bow. Since there was no wood on the island, Ione explained, she had pried up planking from the top deck, then used the lumber and nails she salvaged in an attempt to patch the damage.

'And a darned good job she did too,' Rupert said proudly. 'You should have seen her pounding away, using a rock as a hammer.'

'We were hoping to be rescued, of course, to prevent our actually having to put to sea in this leaky tub.' The strain of waiting and watching for a passing boat was reflected in the fatigue on Ione's sunburned face. But Thalassos was far away from all shipping lanes these days. No sign of help had appeared. 'We couldn't stay here any longer. Our food and water were all but gone. We'd have had to try it tonight, as soon as the tide stabilized. It would have meant rowing all the way, provided we could stay afloat. Our propeller was sheared off in the collision. Rupert's been trying to fashion a pair of oars from more of the deck planking. Even with only one good arm he did a wonderful job—but I'm very relieved we won't have to use them, after all.'

Kelsey remembered what Michael had said about his sister and brother-in-law the first time they met. If their own marriage turned out to be half as strong as the one uniting Ione and Rupert, she thought, they were due to be ecstatically happy.

'How the devil did you find us?' Rupert was asking.

Michael grinned. 'Persistence. And a good bit of help from your daughter.'

Tears filled Ione's eyes. 'We've missed Zoe so much. Half the time all we talked about was getting home to the States and being a family again.'

Both she and Rupert were overjoyed to learn that they would have to go only as far as Mykonos to accomplish that goal. 'Imagine her remembering the details of that map!' Ione marveled. 'Oh, but, Michael, it was so risky to bring her back to Greece. Or for you and Kelsey to become involved in this at all. An utterly ruthless man has been tracking every move we made.'

Only moments before being struck down by the speeding car, Alec Westerlin had whispered the name of Huntley Van Ryn to Rupert. 'He was right to be afraid, poor soul,' Ione added with a shudder. 'That man will stop at nothing to get his hands on the objects that were smuggled into Greece inside that trunk.'

Rather than go into details, Michael just admitted that they had also had their run-ins with Mr Van Ryn and his gang of cutthroats. 'I'm amazed that we've managed to outmaneuver them this long,' he said frankly. 'All the odds are on his side, I'm afraid.'

'Well, he isn't going to win,' Rupert said with determination. 'As soon as we get back to civilization, we intend to turn everything we know over to the Greek authorities. We hadn't wanted to do it that way—'

'But it's all we can think of,' Ione conceded. 'The government can send policemen— soldiers, if necessary. As soon as the problems of ownership get straightened out, the antiquities will be placed in a museum where the whole world can enjoy them. I'll admit we wanted the satisfaction of making the discovery ourselves, but this seems the only way to thwart Huntley Van Ryn's ambitions. If he were to grab the treasure, it would disappear forever.'

'Whatever you've decided is okay with us,' Michael said. 'We can talk about the details on the way back to Mykonos. Right now I just want to get out of here. There's likely to be nothing left of Thalassos to excavate if that volcano down on Santorini starts putting on the show seismologists are predicting.'

Rupert had been staring out to sea, over his brother-in-law's shoulder. 'That sounds ominous,' he said quietly, 'but I'm afraid we have another dilemma confronting us first.'

CHAPTER TEN

Spinning around to follow Rupert's gaze, Kelsey felt her spirits plummet. Half a mile out an elegant yacht had anchored, blockading the island's western approach. Already, a small, fast launch had been lowered from the larger vessel and was speeding shoreward.

Shielding her eyes, she counted three men aboard. Two, worse luck, she had already met. The wheel was being handled by the same taciturn seaman who had shuttled Sarah and her out to the *Naiad* the previous morning. Braced watchfully behind him stood a brawny, dark-haired man. The automatic weapon he clutched looked quite natural in his menacing grip.

'Careful, everybody,' she murmured. 'I doubt that Geoff would hesitate to shoot if any of us gave him the slightest excuse.'

With his good arm Rupert drew his wife closer. 'That character seated in solitary splendor at the back of the launch is Huntley Van Ryn. This quest must really be important to him. Usually he stays aloof and lets others do the dirty work for him.'

'You notice he has a muscleman with an Uzi

186

to handle any minor details like bloodshed.' There was a bitter twinge to Michael's comment. 'As usual, all the breaks are on their side. They've plenty of daylight left to accomplish what they've come to do. And, unlike us, they won't be bothered by that rogue tide. Having just gone out, it'll be hours before it starts to turn.'

Kelsey laced her fingers through his, sharing his disappointment. After all they had been through, it was humiliating to be trapped so effortlessly. 'How did they manage to follow us without once appearing on the horizon? The *Naiad* should have been visible from a long way off.'

The solution to this riddle was soon forthcoming. The man lounging at the stern of the approaching launch raised a loud-hailer to his lips, eliminating the need to strain his throat when communicating. 'My sympathies on your mishap,' he called in a tone that seemed to gloat rather than commiserate. 'It gave us a bad half hour when your blip disappeared off our radar screen. Now I see that you decided to become part of the landscape.'

'Radar!' Kelsey snapped her fingers in quick understanding. 'That means they were following us blind, staying well back so as not to spook us. But, Michael, if they couldn't see us, they must think—'

'That this is *our* boat!' His expressive brown eyes held a new flicker of hope as he glanced

187

toward the battered vessel. 'They can't see the bay on the other side of Zeus's Marbles. With the four of us gathered around this hulk, they must figure we all just cracked up together a little while ago.'

'Well, if that was the case, we wouldn't have had time to make repairs. Ione,' Kelsey said urgently, 'drape that towel you're holding across the motorboat's bow. See if it will cover the spot you worked so hard to patch.'

Ione tossed the beach towel to her right with a strategically aimed flip. It fluttered down to conceal all but one corner of the makeshift repair. They had no chance to rearrange it. The helmsman cut his engine and steered the launch into an expert glide, bringing it the last few yards through the shallows. In a blur of movement Geoff swung out, then reached back to steady the vessel while his employer alighted.

Michael took advantage of their momentary preoccupation to take two quick steps to his right. His casual stance now camouflaged the boarded-over spot on the motorboat's bow. 'We just got here, remember,' he muttered a warning. '*All* of us.'

'Hmmm, the pair of you don't look quite as ratty as we do, but that swim helped,' Rupert drawled whimsically. 'I'm afraid even Robinson Crusoe's Friday would take one look at us all and run.'

Since their arrival Kelsey had not heard so

much as a birdcall. Having grown used to the island's eerie silence, she jumped when sound burst raucously forth from the launch. Left to his own devices, the seaman remaining below had snapped on the radio. Not a person who enjoyed the tranquillity of his own thoughts, she decided. Jangly music had been blaring from the boat she and Sarah had stepped into at the Mykonos wharf too—the boat she'd stolen and sent on its merry way.

She gulped, watching the pair's steady uphill approach. In every way, they seemed to be complete opposites. Geoff's walk was a hulking swagger. Huntley Van Ryn moved with the smooth grace of a thoroughbred.

His appearance certainly was aristocratic, Kelsey had to admit. Beneath the smart yachtsman's hat, a rich vein of silver blazed through his full head of burnished chestnut hair. His skin was tanned, a striking contrast against the immaculate white linen of his beautifully tailored slacks and jacket. It would have given her great pleasure to see him slip and muddy that spotless attire, but his footing, like his ensemble, was impeccable.

Sardonic amusement lurked in his gaze, as if he knew exactly what she'd been hoping and was happy to thwart her wish. The gray eyes grew sterner as they moved to Ione, then flickered in contempt across the torn landscape of Thalassos.

'What a pitiful remnant of land!' he scoffed.

'How could any person with a sense of aesthetics entrust antiquities worth a king's ransom to a plebeian locale such as this?'

'Plebeian? Hardly,' Ione countered in a cool, lecture-hall tone. 'According to all accounts, this island was once under the special protection of Aphrodite, the goddess of love and beauty.'

'Legend was what kept the masses quiet when they had nothing else,' Van Ryn sneered. 'Fortunately, the most talented artisans of the time seemed to take those myths seriously. Many of the exquisite sculptures and paintings they created as tributes to those so-called gods and goddesses are now prized parts of my personal collection. I have made it my life's work to see that each piece is accorded the perfect surroundings it deserves.'

Kelsey wondered if Van Ryn was totally sane. Yesterday Geoff had mentioned his employer's admiration of beauty. But to her it sounded as if his warped attitude went far beyond mere appreciation. The acquisition of glorious works of art had become a mania, an obsession for him. Sad to say, his reference to 'antiquities worth a king's ransom' made it clear what it was he hoped to acquire here on Thalassos.

'Now,' he continued in a high, demanding voice, 'you can save us all a great deal of unpleasantness by pointing out the cave that was the site of these ancient superstitions.'

Rupert faked an expressive shrug, though it must have caused his injured shoulder a great deal of pain. 'Look around, man! The cave you're talking about is probably at the bottom of the sea. This island has been twisted out of all recognition!'

'And it's doubtful that even this much of Thalassos will survive much longer,' Michael added significantly. 'News bulletins have been clogging the airwaves the entire day. Nea Kameni is steaming. Seismologists are urging the evacuation of Santorini. That's only a few miles south of here. One more good shake and this island is likely to be just a memory.'

'Like that place Atlantis. It sank like a rock, boss. I saw a TV special about it once.' The man standing behind Van Ryn shuffled uneasily as he made the comment.

At first Kelsey had considered Geoff the coldblooded type of hooligan who would never flinch at anything, so long as he held a gun in his hand. Now she revised her original opinion. Sarah's 'gentleman friend' had no desire to pit his own brute strength and the power of his Uzi against the forces of nature.

Geoff's anxious glance assessed the devastated landscape, then shifted to the *Naiad*, riding placidly at anchor. 'That Nico is a landlubber,' he groused. 'If there's trouble brewing, he couldn't begin to handle the yacht by himself.'

Van Ryn cast him a flinty look. 'It was your

suggestion to leave most of the crew back in Mykonos. You persuaded me that the four of us could handle this particular errand ourselves.'

'Well, haven't we? It's working out fine—*and* without a lot of witnesses!' Geoff gave a malevolent grin. 'Now that we know which island that old man stashed the museum loot on, we can come back and get it later, after the volcano calms down and it's safe to go poking around. For now, I say let's dispose of this bunch and head on back to the *Naiad* before anything happens.'

'Coward! Can't you see they're simply trying to scare us away?' Van Ryn peered around the torn-up plateau, as if determined to discover what he had come for in spite of his henchman's trepidation.

But Kelsey noticed he hadn't objected to Geoff's suggestion that they be shot, only to leaving immediately. Their minutes were running out. If only she could persuade Van Ryn that keeping them alive for even a short while longer was in his own best interests, they might get some reinforcement from that noise junkie down in the launch. Any time now another news bulletin might break into his station, reaffirming the truth of Michael's claim.

'I've heard of all sorts of islands disappearing after a monstrous explosion,' she spoke up, building on Geoff's reference to

Atlantis. 'Thousands of people in Java and Sumatra were killed when Krakatoa erupted in 1883. Some of the places where they lived were totally vaporized and never seen again. But it's kind of funny. Other islands popped up out of nowhere.'

That got their attention. Kelsey hoped she sounded so sure of her subject that the two men she was trying to impress would never guess that the last of those details had been made up out of thin air. 'That might happen with Thalassos too,' she got to the crux of the message she was trying to put across. 'Of course, even if this island were to completely emerge again, its hillsides would be honeycombed with caves. It would take an expert to figure out which was the right one.'

'That's enough out of you,' Geoff growled, his finger tightening over the Uzi's trigger. 'You're the cause of us losing a perfectly good motorboat. Do you think you're gonna get us killed now, talking us into sticking around here until that volcano blows to see if this island goes up or down?'

Van Ryn silenced him with a sharp look. But he, too, seemed irate when he recalled what a nuisance Kelsey had made of herself the previous day. 'You have presented an intriguing possibility, Miss Anderson. Unfortunately for you and two of your companions, we need only one expert. Professor Strasse can act as our guide should

Thalassos once more emerge from the depths.'

'Not me,' said Ione, who knew perfectly well Kelsey had concocted that story about islands popping up out of nowhere. 'I wouldn't be any help to you without the others. Each of us has a piece of the puzzle that the others don't know. It's a—a safeguard. That way no one could jump in ahead of time and grab the whole prize.'

Michael had been poised to attack the gunman with his bare hands if Geoff had made one more menacing move toward his fiancée. Now, watching the speculative way their adversaries glanced at each other, he relaxed slightly. They didn't believe Ione, not really. But there was always a chance in a thousand that she might be telling the truth.

'What she said makes sense to them because they would have taken the very same precautions themselves,' he muttered into Kelsey's ear.

Their fate was in the lap of the gods now, she thought. Her fingers tightened around Michael's as they waited for Huntley Van Ryn to make the decision as to whether they lived or died. If this was to be their last moment together, she wanted him to know that her final thoughts had been about him.

At that exact instant a thunderous roar boomed forth from the earth. Beneath their feet, the ground jolted and began to shift. Ten yards away, a crevasse split the pebbled soil of the plateau into jagged halves, then slammed it back together again.

The shaking increased. The two couples clung to each other as the echoing rumble drummed on and on and on. Geoff was thrown off balance by the sickening motion underfoot. The weapon he'd been holding landed with a splat as he struggled to keep from toppling over. But none of the four people who'd been threatened by the gun made a try to snatch it out of his reach. A more terrifying threat stood poised to menace their safety.

'Look out!'

The cry came from Rupert as halfway up the craggy peak the immense boulder to which the motorboat had been tied began to shudder its way out of the ground. He and Ione dived out of its steamrollering path, with Kelsey and Michael right behind them. The wooden prow splintered into toothpicks in that first grinding impact, then boat and rock went over the edge together, flipping end over end, like acrobats somersaulting in tandem. Crashing, ricocheting, rending apart down the entire slope to the water.

As if that cacophony had been too much for even the elements to tolerate, the ground stilled. The trembling air caught its breath. In the stunned silence that followed, not one of the six people on the slope uttered a sound. Even the launch's stentorian music had ceased, leaving a void that made Kelsey's ears ache with its surreal emptiness.

Five, perhaps six heartbeats thudded past before noise broke out from the radio again. Not the rhythmic tintinnabulation that had been blasting forth earlier, but words, reeling so excitedly off their speaker's tongue that they tripped over each other in their haste to be spoken. Only 'Nea Kameni' was decipherable to Kelsey. But from the ghastly pallor spreading across Geoff's face, it was clear that he, like her three companions, had understood every syllable.

'*Now* will you listen to reason?' He all but hurled a translation at Huntley Van Ryn. 'They called that thing a tremor. A warning. It only reached 5.1 on the Richter scale, that idiot on the radio said. The volcano has barely started warming up. Scientists predict something worse before it finally blows its top!'

'You've made your point,' Van Ryn conceded grimly. 'We'll return to the safety of the *Naiad* for the time being.'

Along with all the other emotions surging through her consciousness, Kelsey was aware of a faint twinge of satisfaction at the sight of the billionaire. He had lost his hat in the excitement, and the muddy progress of the boulder on its crashing downhill course had sullied his white linen suit with dozens of speckles and stains.

Then sun glinted off the Uzi's cold steel finish. Survival became her only concern.

196

'What about them?' Geoff demanded, fingering the weapon.

That chance in a thousand that Ione might have been telling the truth was more than Van Ryn cared to risk. 'Leave them,' he ordered. 'They can hardly swim all the way to Ios, and if future quakes do lift this pitiful excuse of an island out of the sea once again, I want them alive long enough to locate that cave for me. Get going! This filthy place makes me sick!'

Watching the pair skid their way down to where the launch waited, its motor already purring, Kelsey breathed a prayer of thanksgiving for the reprieve they had been granted. For the first time since spotting the intruders, she gave a thought to the fishing boat. Snug, she hoped, in the wide harbor beyond the ridge of boulders. Unlike the gigantic rock that had come crashing down atop the motorboat, Zeus's Marbles had swayed but remained in place. Geoff and Van Ryn had come and gone, never realizing that an escape route from Thalassos for their prey waited just beyond the line of rocks.

They could make a run for it as soon as darkness descended and trust that the tide would hold, that none of the villains aboard the *Naiad* would be monitoring the radar screen. Though their future was by no means secure, Kelsey felt tears of gratitude course down her face as she wrapped her arms around Michael.

'We're alive,' she murmured. 'Together.'

Love glowed in his eyes. He brushed a fleck of mud off her forehead, then pressed his lips to the spot. 'Alive and together,' he echoed. 'Thanks to that inspiration of yours about this island popping to the surface again.'

'Embellished by my wife's convincing bluff,' Rupert added fondly. 'Honey, you half convinced those cut-throats that we were every bit as corrupt as—Ione! What's the matter?'

Rigid with horror, she was pointing out to sea. 'Good heavens—they'll be swallowed alive!'

Kelsey had time for only one appalled look. Then Michael was hauling her upward, shouting for the others to run. 'Climb as high as you can! That thing's at least thirty feet tall and gathering force. There's no guarantee it won't veer in our direction!'

But by the time they'd climbed halfway up the craggy peak, they could no longer keep their eyes off the riveting spectacle. The tumultuous forces of nature that had caused the earthquake had churned the Aegean into a frenzy. Well out to sea, a monumental tidal wave raced across the surface, gaining vigor and velocity with every pulsebeat.

'I saw something like that once in Japan,' Rupert said in awe. 'They call it a *tsunami*. Nothing in its path will stand a chance.'

Almost before the words had died away, the destructive wall of water overtook the speeding launch. With crushing force the torrent sluiced over the boat and its doomed occupants, then bore onward toward the *Naiad*. As long as she lived, Kelsey knew she would never forget the sight of that beautiful white ship teetering like an exploded champagne cork atop the foamy crest. The next instant the *tsunami* had hurled the yacht into the reef with battering-ram power.

'Papa used to say that a storm at sea was caused by Poseidon shaking his fist,' Michael said, his voice filled with awe.

Shaking his fist and flexing his muscles, Kelsey thought, shuddering as the *Naiad* burst against the teeth of the rocks and exploded into a thousand pieces. 'Just before the earthquake hit, I remember thinking that our fate was in the lap of the gods.' She tore her eyes away from the vessel's death throes. 'It's hard not to wonder, isn't it, whether—whether somehow those scornful remarks Huntley Van Ryn made about myth and the so-called gods and goddesses could have been overheard?'

*   *   *

Kelsey Anderson and Michael Devos were married a few days later in the ancient Byzantine church at Daphni. Once again a small seaplane waited down the coast. Its journey was happily postponed for a few hours while family and friends joined in to celebrate the festive occasion.

Following the ceremony, luncheon was served on an outdoor terrace across the green, where tables had been set up beneath a latticework canopy. Luscious grapes and fat green leaves threaded back and forth among the lath, shading the guests from the hot sun. There was dancing, Greek style, with handkerchiefs threaded between people's fingers. Meeting Michael's gaze as they spun around in a circle, Kelsey knew he did not intend to be kept at arm's length very much longer.

At last the cake was cut, toasts were drunk, and the bouquet tossed directly into Joanna's outstretched fingers. With a smile that promised her groom she would not be gone long, Kelsey went inside to change from her wedding gown to a dress more suitable for traveling.

Her new sister-in-law came along. 'How romantic! A honeymoon on Capri,' Ione said with a reminiscent sigh. 'Still, I'm surprised the two of you aren't tired of islands by now.'

'We weren't castaways like you and Rupert for days and days and days, remember?' Kelsey smiled and snapped the clasp of the necklace Michael had given her. It matched the wide gold band she now wore on her left hand. 'Besides, we also plan to visit Florence and Venice and Rome before flying home to Seattle. Actually, though, anyplace—except

Thalassos—would seem delightful, so long as we were seeing it together.'

Through the window she caught sight of the monastery wall, built long ago with materials taken from the ancient sanctuary of Apollo.

'Ione,' she said thoughtfully, 'there was too much else to think about that day Nea Kameni spent its force on a tidal wave instead of staging a full-scale eruption, but I *have* wondered. While you were marooned, did you ever find your way into the cave where Rupert's ancestor cached the contents of his steamer trunk at Aphrodite's shrine?'

'Not exactly *in*. I must admit catching a glimpse, just to satisfy my curiosity. With that, our quest was completed. But we've decided to pass the glory of discovery along to the next generation. In another two or three decades Zoe will be an enthusiastic archaeologist with a brilliant future ahead of her. Chances are, she'll have cousins who are also interested in exploring ancient sites ... and finding something unexpected.'

Those cousins Ione spoke of would be her own children, Kelsey mused. Hers and Michael's. From infancy they would be taught Greek along with English and told bedtime stories about all the old traditions.

'What a wonderful idea! Thalassos is the last place anyone would dream of looking for Priam's treasure, now that Huntley Van Ryn and his henchmen are out of the picture forever.' She smiled at her sister-in-law, thinking of how a boulder had swayed when her arm grazed it. 'Maybe the four of us can go along. Give them a little parental advice about the easiest way to push Zeus's Marbles aside . . ..'

We hope you have enjoyed this Large Print book. Other Chivers Press or G. K. Hall Large Print books are available at your library or directly from the publishers. For more information about current and forthcoming titles, please call or write, without obligation, to:

Chivers Press Limited
Windsor Bridge Road
Bath BA2 3AX
England
Tel. (01225) 335336

OR

G. K. Hall
P.O. Box 159
Thorndike, Maine 04986
USA
Tel. (800) 223–6121 (U.S. & Canada)
In Maine call collect: (207) 948–2962

All our Large Print titles are designed for easy reading, and all our books are made to last.